## "Carrie," Frank said, his voice husky

"Yes?"

"I'm going to kiss you."

"I wish you would." Her voice was none too steady either.

He lifted her chin with the backs of his fingers and she closed her eyes as he bent toward her. The first touch of his lips was a tentative brushing against hers.

She loved his lips. They were warm, full, gentle.

Then he gathered her into his arms and deepened the kiss. He groaned and put his heart and soul into it, and she responded in kind.

Dear Lord, he was so fine. She clutched handfuls of his shirt to keep from puddling at his feet. She was just getting started when he broke away.

"I really enjoyed the evening," he said. He dropped a quick kiss on her forehead instead of on the lips she blatantly offered. "Good night."

And then he was gone. Out the door faster than greased lightning.

She lifted her eyebrows and stared at the door that had closed behind him. "And good night to you, too, Judge."

Dear Reader,

This is the second of three books about a family of tall, dark and handsome fellows, the Texas Outlaws. In keeping with family tradition, the Outlaw brothers are named for famous desperadoes and are in law enforcement and public service. I hope that last month you read and enjoyed the first book of the miniseries, about J. J. (Jesse James) Outlaw, sheriff of Naconiche (NAK-uh-KNEE-chee) County, Texas. This story is about his older brother, Frank James Outlaw—who wouldn't vote for a judge with that name?

Again set in the tall-timbered, rolling hills of the fictitious small county seat of Naconiche, this tale features more of the colorful characters typical of small East Texas towns around where I was born—warm, welcoming and often a shade eccentric. East Texas is where the Old South meets the West, so there's a mix of cowboys and country folks, and most people are friendly—but a few still live in the backwoods, guard their privacy as if they were still moonshinin' and tote shotguns to ward off strangers.

When Carrie Campbell blew into town, she never imagined that she would meet and come to love so many people—especially a judge with a pair of rambunctious twins. But magical things seem to happen when you stay at the Twilight Inn. Come along and see.

Warmest regards!

*Jan Hudson*

# THE JUDGE
## Jan Hudson

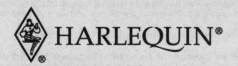

HARLEQUIN®

TORONTO • NEW YORK • LONDON
AMSTERDAM • PARIS • SYDNEY • HAMBURG
STOCKHOLM • ATHENS • TOKYO • MILAN • MADRID
PRAGUE • WARSAW • BUDAPEST • AUCKLAND

ISBN 0-373-75025-0

THE JUDGE

Copyright © 2004 by Janece Hudson.

www.eHarlequin.com

**Printed in U.S.A.**

For Mary Hudson
And with special thanks, for Marilyn Jefferies Meehan,
attorney and former landman.

# Chapter One

Still steamed, Carrie Campbell yanked open the door and strode into the justice of the peace's offices. It had chapped her good when that moon-faced Gomer had given her a speeding ticket not two minutes after she'd crossed the county line. Doing seventy-one in a fifty-mile-an-hour zone, he'd informed her in a nasal drawl. She hadn't seen a different speed posted. How could she be held accountable when a humongous semi parked on the shoulder had clearly blocked the sign? She'd gone back and looked.

She ought to fight it. Everything in her screamed to go to the mat about this. But she needed to play it low-key around Naconiche County, Texas—at least until her business here was finished. She could just hear her uncle Tuck saying, "Get down off your high horse, girl, and pay the damned ticket. Play your hand close to your vest and don't stir up the locals. Remember you've got a job to do."

Carrie stopped, took a deep breath and forced herself to relax. She couldn't let her temper screw up things.

Okay. She'd pay the damned ticket—if she could

find somebody to take her money. Nobody was sitting at the front desk.

Spotting a door ajar at the back of the large anteroom, she headed straight for it. The sooner she got this over with, the sooner she could get on with her plans.

Horace P. Pfannepatter, Justice of the Peace, Precinct 2 was painted in black letters on the frosted glass panel. Through the crack, she could see a dark-haired man in a white shirt and tie sitting at a desk, rummaging through a drawer.

She rapped on the glass and pushed open the door. "Judge?"

"Yes," he said, glancing up.

Stunned, for a moment she could only gawk. The judge was drop-dead, movie-star gorgeous. He had big brown eyes with eyelashes a foot long and one of those perfectly sculpted faces she'd only seen on young Greek men. She hated to admit it, but the guy took her breath away.

A pity about the name.

Who could seriously consider anyone named Horace P. Pfannepatter?

"What does the P. stand for?"

He stared at her in a sort of slack-jawed way that made Carrie wonder if his mother had married her first cousin. Mostly his eyes seemed to zero in on her bare legs. From his expression, you'd have thought he'd never seen a woman in shorts before. She yanked off her sunglasses and tapped her foot impatiently.

His eyes finally made it back to her face, and he gave himself a little shake. "Pardon?"

"What does the P. stand for?" she said a little louder, thinking maybe he had a hearing problem.

He gave her another out-to-lunch look, then frowned. "The P.?"

Despite his good looks, this guy didn't seem to be the sharpest knife in the drawer. What did it take to get elected to JP around here—being able to sit up and take nourishment?

"The P. in Horace P. Pfannepatter. What does it stand for?"

"Oh. Puffer. It's a family name."

Figured. A real shame. A real shame, too, about the gold wedding ring he wore.

"Your eyes are…very unusual," he said, squinting at her. "I—I suppose you hear that a lot."

She smiled. "A lot."

After a slow trip down her body, his gaze went back to her legs. She almost reconsidered paying the ticket. Twenty to one that with a little sweet talk, she could get Horace to dismiss it, especially with the photo of the sign and the parked semi she had taken— and given his preoccupation with her exposed skin.

Better not. Resigned to her earlier decision, she sighed. "I need to pay a ticket."

"A ticket? Oh. Maureen can help you with that."

"Maureen?"

"Yes. At the desk out front."

"Nobody was there when I came in."

"Let's see if we can find her," he said, standing.

If Carrie thought he looked good sitting, on his feet he was dynamite. He must have been six-two or -three and no slouch in the body department. When he touched her back to usher her from his office, she felt as if she'd been zapped with a cattle prod.

Odd.

Static electricity, she was sure. He was *married* for goshsakes.

He smiled and her knees wobbled. He had a mouth full of perfect white teeth and a killer of a lopsided smile. "Ah, there's Maureen. She can help you."

A middle-aged blonde, with a half inch of black roots, stood, a distressed look on her face. "Oh, Judge, I'm sorry. I was in the storeroom looking for another box."

"No problem. This lady needs to pay a ticket."

"Yes, sir. Here's the one I found." Maureen handed him an empty carton.

"Thanks. This is perfect."

The judge went back to his office, and Carrie shelled out eighty-seven bucks to Maureen. The ticket paid, she hightailed it toward the Twilight Inn. She was tired and thirsty and eager to get settled in at the place that would be home for a while.

FRANK OUTLAW, judge of the County Court-at-Law of Naconiche County, stood at the window, absently fingering his wedding ring as he watched the white BMW pull away. He couldn't believe that the woman had shaken him the way she had. He hadn't experienced that kind of mind-blowing reaction to a woman since he was a teenager—probably not since he'd first kissed Susan when they were about fourteen. He hadn't even thought about a woman in sexual terms since his wife died, and that had been two years before.

But something about the dark-haired, purple-eyed vixen who had just strolled into Horace's office had sure revved up his motor. He'd been so dumbfounded that he hadn't been able to string a coherent sentence together. She probably thought he was a blithering idiot.

He'd always been a leg man, and she'd had the longest, prettiest legs he'd ever seen. Hell, she was gorgeous all over. Tall and slender with those startling eyes and kiss-me lips, she was a knockout. Not even the slightly crooked front tooth or the small scar on the side of her chin detracted from her looks. In fact, the small imperfections only seemed to make her more intriguing and heighten her sensuality. And she was sexy. It oozed from her skin and clung to her like a cloud of low morning fog on the river bottom. He was getting aroused just thinking about her. It was a strange feeling.

Frank chuckled to himself. Good thing his brother J.J. wasn't around, or he'd never hear the end of it. J.J. was always after him to take out this woman or that, eager to jump-start his sex life, but Frank simply hadn't been interested. Susan had been the love of his life, and when she'd been killed, something had died in Frank as well.

Good thing, too, that the woman was probably passing through on her way to someplace besides Naconiche. A woman like her could deal a man some misery.

There was a rap on the door, and Maureen stuck in her head. "I'm sorry about the interruption, Judge. That's the third ticket Otis Purvis has issued in the same spot today. And there's a truck broken down on the side of the highway blocking the sign. I noticed it on my way to work this morning. I told Miss Campbell she had a right to appeal, but she insisted on paying the ticket."

"Miss Campbell?"

"Carolyn Campbell. From Houston. But she's staying at the Twilight Inn while she's in town. I gave her directions."

Frank felt his gut twist. The Twilight Inn was the motel run by his soon to be sister-in-law, Mary Beth Parker. It was on his way home. He nodded. "I have to be back at the courthouse by two, and I need to get a move on. I'll be through packing up here in a few minutes, Maureen, and I'll take Horace's things to Ida."

"I'm sure she appreciates that."

"It's the least I can do for an old friend, and I know Fletcher is anxious to move in and get started."

"Things just won't be the same without Horace around," Maureen said. "He'd been JP since I was a kid."

"I know. We'll all miss him."

Maureen went back to her desk, and Frank went back to packing. He tried his best to keep his mind off Carolyn Campbell and her legs. He didn't have much luck.

CARRIE FOUND the Twilight Inn without any problem. It was an old-fashioned motel, but it seemed quite neat and charming with its new coat of paint and window boxes filled with red geraniums. There was a sign on a nearby building identifying The Twilight Tearoom. She hoped the food was good. She'd missed lunch, and she was famished. Pulling to a stop in front of the unit that looked like an office, she got out and went inside.

Four old guys sat at a card table playing dominoes. All of them gave her the once-over, and one rose when she entered. "Hep ya?" he said, walking to the counter and giving her a big denture smile.

"I'm Carrie Campbell. I have a reservation."

"Yes sir-ree bob. I've got you right here in the book. You're in number five. I'm Will, and these fellers are Curtis, B.D. and Howard. We're the biggest part of the staff of the Twilight Inn." He produced a key. "If you'll sign the register, B.D. will get your bags." He handed her a pen.

"I can handle my luggage, but thanks anyhow."

"No problem. All part of the service. And B.D. is stronger than he looks."

"I'm fit as a fiddle," one of the other old gents said, standing.

B.D. looked as if a strong gust of wind would blow him to Oklahoma. Torn between not wanting to hurt the old man's pride and her fear that lifting her bags might give him a heart attack, she finally smiled and said, "Thanks."

"Glad to oblige," B.D. said, beaming. She'd made the right choice.

"I'd like to get something to eat," Carrie said. "Is the restaurant open?"

One of the other men at the table glanced at the clock and shook his head. "The tearoom's only open from eleven to one, so it's been closed for more'n half an hour, but I reckon Mary Beth's still in the kitchen. I 'spect she could rustle up a bite for you. Let me run and ask her." He took off at a spry clip.

The fourth old man stood. "I'm Howard, and I'll give B.D. a hand with the bags. You planning on staying long?"

"I may be here for several weeks," Carrie said. "I'm a genealogist, and I'm researching several lines in this area." The lie rolled easily off her tongue. It was best if the word didn't get out too soon that she was a landman for an oil company and interested in leasing acreage in the area, or she'd find competition sniffing around. To keep things quiet until she was ready to make offers, she frequently posed as a professional genealogist, and in fact had done some real research as a hobby.

"That so?" B.D. said. "You ought to talk to Millie down at the library. She knows about all there is to know about the town history and the early settlers."

"Thanks, I'll do that."

B.D. squinted at her. "I swear. I just noticed your eyes are purple."

She laughed. "Actually, they're more violet."

"Now that you mention it, I believe you're right. Puts me to mind of that actress, you know, the one that's been married so many times. Anyhow, they're right pretty."

"Thanks, B.D. Shall we get the bags?"

"You just pull your car into the slot beside number five," Howard said, "and we'll have you unloaded in a jiffy. I'll go ahead and turn on the air conditioner. It won't take but a minute to cool off the place. I swear you'd think that it ought to be cooler being the first of October. I guess it's that global warming."

In no time the men had everything unloaded and the room cooling. She was surprised at the accommodations. In her line of work, she'd stayed in some real dumps, but this room was bright and cheerful. The walls were a soft peach and the spread on the double bed was a muted plaid of peach, yellow and green that matched the draperies. Pleasant framed watercolors decorated the walls and an overstuffed green chair and ottoman looked quite comfy.

Howard put her laptop on the desk, which would be perfect for working. "Bathroom's through there," he said, indicating a back corner of the large room. "And over there," he said, nodding to an alcove in the other corner, "is what we call the kitchenette. It has a microwave, a coffeepot and a little refrigerator. You can fix a bite of breakfast here in the mornings, or if you've a mind for something more substantial, the City Grill is the place to go. Everything you need to know about places to eat is in that little brochure on the desk."

"There's a map of town in there, too," B.D. told her. "Not that you're likely to get lost. Just stop and ask anybody for directions to where you want to go. Naconiche is a right friendly place."

There was a rap on the open door, and an attractive blond woman with a tray came in. "Hi, Carrie. I'm Mary Beth Parker, owner of the Twilight Inn and Tearoom. I've brought you soup and a sandwich and some raspberry tea. I hope you like avocado."

"I adore avocado," Carrie said, smiling. "Thanks for rescuing a starving woman."

"No problem." Mary Beth set the tray on the small table near the microwave. "Welcome to Naconiche, Carrie. Curtis tells me that you're going to be with us for several weeks."

"She's one of them genealogists," B.D. said.

"How fascinating," Mary Beth said. "I'd love to hear more about it sometime, but I'm sure you'd like to have your lunch and get settled in now. My daughter and I live in the apartment behind the office, so call if you need anything."

"I will. Thanks."

"Come on, guys," Mary Beth said, hustling the old men from the room, "let's leave Carrie in peace."

Carrie smiled as she closed the door behind them. She liked Mary Beth immediately. They were about the same age, and she suspected that given different circumstances, they might become friends. For sure, Mary Beth would be a valuable source of information.

From the time she'd rolled into the city limits, Carrie had felt good vibes in this little jerk-water town. Strange, since she was a city girl through and through. Maybe it was because she could smell oil hidden in the hills and hollows. Or maybe it was something else. In any case, she had a hunch—and her hunches were always dead-on—that this assignment was going to be different from all the others.

As she lifted the napkin from the food tray, her thoughts went briefly to Judge Horace P. Pfannepatter. Too bad he was married.

# Chapter Two

Carrie couldn't function without her morning jolt of caffeine, and there was no way of getting the can open short of chewing it off with her teeth. And she was tempted to try that. She spat out a few colorful phrases and threw the recalcitrant can opener across the room. The blasted thing didn't work. All she'd managed to do was puncture the coffee can and let out a *whoosh* of aroma that ran her crazy.

Her frustration level was off the charts. In spite of stocking up on a few breakfast items the afternoon before, it looked like the City Grill for her. She hoped they opened early. After dressing quickly in jeans and a pullover, she grabbed her briefcase and tore off toward the square of the small town.

The café was doing a brisk business. Only two seats at the counter were available. She commandeered one of them and stowed her briefcase between her feet.

"What'll it be, honey?" asked the pint-size waitress who held a steaming carafe.

"Coffee," Carrie said. "Quick."

The waitress laughed, and the web of lines around her eyes put her age closer to sixty than forty. "One

of them mornings, huh? I've had a few of them myself.'' She slipped a mug onto the counter and poured
in one practiced motion. "Cream?"

"No. Black is fine."

"I'll be back when you've had time to rev your
motor.'' The waitress turned to an elderly man who'd
taken the stool next to hers and poured a mug for
him. "Morning, Mr. Murdock. Haven't seen you
around for a few days."

"Good morning, Vera. I've been in Dallas. I returned last night."

"Have you heard about Horace Pfannepatter?"

Carrie's ears perked up, and she glanced toward the
two.

The old man, who was wearing a suit and a red
bow tie, nodded gravely. "Yes, I had a message on
my machine. Sad business. And him in his prime. I'm
sure Ida must be devastated. I plan to call on her this
morning."

"She's pretty broke up. Them two was real close,
and I don't know what she'll do without him.'' Vera
turned to Carrie. "Hon, have you decided what you'll
have to go along with that coffee?"

Carrie hadn't given food any thought. Was that *her*
Horace Pfannepatter they were talking about? "Uh,
I'll have a toasted bagel."

Vera gave her a toothy grin. "You're not likely to
find any bagels around here—unless they carry some
frozen ones over at Bullock's Grocery. Closest thing
I can offer you is a short stack."

"That's fine," Carrie said, her mind still not on
food. "Excuse me for eavesdropping, but I heard you
talking about Horace Pfannepatter. Is he the one
who's justice of the peace?"

"Vera!" a male voice called from a booth in the rear. "Could we have another round of coffee back here?"

"You and Frank keep your britches on, J.J. I'll be there in a minute," she blared, then she nodded to Carrie and said quietly, "The very one. Keeled over with a heart attack real sudden."

"And *died?*"

"Deader 'n a doornail." Vera topped Carrie's coffee and took off at a fast clip, shouting as she strode, "Gimme a short stack, Lonnie, and a number three over easy."

Carrie was too stunned to do anything but stare after the waitress. She couldn't believe that the good-looking JP had died. He'd looked so…*healthy* when she saw him yesterday. She felt a sudden and aching loss—and she barely knew the man. The thought of pancakes made her stomach turn over. She drank her coffee quickly, slapped a bill on the counter and fled with her briefcase.

She decided to buy a new can opener, go back to her room and start the morning over. Horace stayed on her mind the entire time she searched Bullock's aisles. His loss haunted her. Crazy, she told herself. She'd only seen the man once in her life…but somehow he'd made a powerful impression.

FORTIFIED WITH more coffee and a carton of peach yogurt, Carrie went downtown again and parked in front of the old stone courthouse that had probably been built a hundred or more years ago. Three stories tall, the handsome pillared structure was similar to a dozen or two original courthouses still in use in Texas—Texas Renaissance the style was called, a combination of architectural styles popular during the period. Carrie hadn't been in all the 254 county courthouses in the state, but she'd visited a large number of them and she was always glad to see one of the old ones preserved.

The Naconiche courthouse showed community pride of the sort that was responsible for the original construction of the town's heart. Several large trees shaded the grounds and well-tended flower beds flanked the walks. She looked forward to exploring the inside.

A variety of businesses occupied the buildings that faced the square. She noted a couple of antique stores that looked interesting, an ice-cream shop called the Double Dip that she wanted to try out later. Now she needed to familiarize herself with the courthouse, determine where the documents she needed were housed and how the town's records were kept.

As a petroleum landman she first had to find out who owned the property and the mineral rights to the large area that her company wanted to lease. Locating the property owners wasn't too difficult—the county tax roles could tell her that. But frequently the current owners didn't own all the mineral rights. Former owners—sometimes two or three sales back—often retained a percentage of the mineral rights on their acreage, usually a half interest. That meant that she had to track down deeds and locate heirs as well as check on any existing leases.

She couldn't afford to make any errors, and the tedious work took a lot of time. But actually, she kind of enjoyed doing the research. It was like working a crossword puzzle.

Inside the courthouse Carrie smelled the familiar

mélange of aging papers, cleaning solutions and the lingering odor of old tobacco smoke. Even though there were No Smoking signs now, years of cigars and cigarettes had infused the walls with the faint distinctive scent common to so many of the courthouses she'd been in. After a tour of the fine old building with its polished marble and rich oak trim, she located the tax office on the second floor, just down the hall from the chambers of the judge of the County Court-at-Law.

Judge Frank J. Outlaw, the brass nameplate beside the door said. She smiled. Outlaw—a peculiar name for a judge.

With a few directions from a clerk, Carrie located the records she wanted to study, took out her minicomputer and a pad and got to work.

CARRIE'S STOMACH growled, and she glanced at her watch. Five of twelve. Her yogurt was a faded memory, and she was hungry. She couldn't believe she'd been working all morning without a break, but as usual she'd gotten absorbed and time had flown by. Stretching, she loosened the kinks in her back, stiff from bending over the papers so long.

Her first thought was to go across the street to the City Grill for lunch, then she decided that the tearoom was a better choice. She packed her briefcase and left the tax office. Not a dozen steps away, her cell phone rang, and she dug through her shoulder bag to retrieve it.

While she was looking, she collided with someone. "Sorry," she said, glancing up.

Her heart lurched, and she could feel the blood leave her face. It was Horace P. Pfannepatter.

"My God," she said. "It can't be. You're dead!"

He smiled. "I don't think so." He looked down at his hands, turning them over and back. "Nope. I seem to have all my working parts. Your phone's ringing."

"But…but the waitress this morning said that you'd had a heart attack and died."

He frowned. "Which waitress?"

"Vera at the café across the street."

"I can't imagine why she would have said that. I had breakfast there this morning with my brother. You'd better get that," he said, pointing to her ringing purse.

Not taking her eyes from his face, she grabbed the phone, said, "I'll call you back," and crammed it back into her bag. "Maybe it was your father they were talking about. Do you have the same name?"

"Nope. My father's name is John Wesley Hardin Outlaw, Wes for short."

"Outlaw? Then…how… Aren't you the JP?"

A slow smile spread over his face. "You thought I was Horace? No, I'm Frank Outlaw." He stuck out his hand.

Bedarned if she didn't feel herself blush as she took his hand. "Carrie Campbell. Sorry that…" She forgot what she was about to say. He had a million-dollar smile. And a kind of charisma that radiated from him and enveloped her in its magnetism.

"Have you had lunch?" he asked.

She shook her head.

"I was on my way to eat during the noon recess. Why don't you join me, and I'll explain about Horace."

"At the City Grill?"

"I'm not too keen on their special today. I'd planned on the Twilight Tearoom. It's not too far."

"I know," Carrie responded. "I'm staying at the motel."

"Of course you are. I remember that Maureen mentioned that."

She drew a blank. "Maureen?"

"The clerk at the JP office."

"Oh, yes. I...uh...need to drop by my room for a minute. Why don't I meet you there?" She suddenly realized that he was still holding her hand, and she withdrew it quickly and started for the stairs.

"Where are you parked?" he asked as they descended.

"By the south entrance."

"And I'm by the north. I'll go ahead and get a table before they're all gone."

"Is the Tearoom a popular place?"

"Very. They have the best food in town."

At the foot of the stairs Carrie's cell phone rang again. "Excuse me," she said. "I suppose I should take this."

He waved and turned down a hall while she answered. It was her uncle Tuck.

"How are things going in the boonies?"

"Going fine. I'm at the courthouse now. I've just stopped for lunch." She continued out the door while she talked.

He asked for some figures from another job, and she promised to e-mail them to him that afternoon.

"Carrie, play this one extra close to your vest. I ran into Wyatt Hearn at the Petroleum Club last night, and he was sniffing around too close for comfort. I'd hate for him to get wind of things and steal this out from under us. You haven't seen any of his boys around town have you?''

Wyatt Hearn was another independent oilman and a bitter rival of her uncle. "Nope. I haven't seen anybody. I'll keep an eye out. Think I should dye my hair and wear a fake nose?''

Uncle Tuck hooted with laughter. "I don't think you have to go that far, darlin'. Just don't let on to anybody why you're there until you're ready to get their names on the dotted line.''

"Gotcha. I'll report in at the end of the week.''

At her car, she tossed her bag and her briefcase onto the seat and climbed in. If she hurried she'd have time to freshen up a bit before lunch. It wasn't often these days that she got to have lunch with a good-looking guy.

*Remember that he's married,* she told herself.

She sighed. For a few minutes she'd forgotten. Wouldn't you know—the first guy who turned her on in ages, and he was taken. Just as well, she told herself. She had work to do and didn't need the distraction.

AS HE DROVE to the tearoom, Frank felt as nervous as a kid on his first date. But it wasn't a *date,* he told himself. It was a simple shared meal. Still, he wondered why in the world he had opened his big mouth and invited her to the tearoom of all places. His brother was bound to be there—along with some of the biggest gossips in Naconiche. His mother and half the town would know that he was eating with a beautiful woman before they finished dessert.

God, what a mess he'd gotten himself into—and all because of an innocent invitation. He didn't like what everybody would be thinking, but one look into those incredible eyes of hers had short-circuited his brain.

He made it to the tearoom just in time to get the last available table. Unfortunately it was in the middle of the room. He sat facing the door so that he could see when Carrie arrived.

"I'll have iced tea for now," he told the young waitress. "Make that two teas. I'm waiting on somebody. It should be just a couple of minutes." He turned to study the menu on the chalkboard over the bar.

"Hey, big brother," a familiar voice said as a chair scraped the floor.

Damn. It was J.J. "What are you doing here?"

J.J. chuckled as he sat down. "What am I doing here? Hell, I eat lunch here almost every day. Half of the time with you. What do you think I'm doing here? Hey, Lori," he said to the waitress who served the tea along with a basket of bread. "I'll have the chicken spaghetti special. What are you having, Frank?"

"I haven't ordered yet."

"Why not?" J.J. picked up one of the tea glasses and took a big swig.

"I'm…waiting on someone. Lori, would you bring another tea?"

"Sure thing, Judge. Be right back."

J.J. frowned and set down the glass he held. "Whoops, have I stepped in a cow patty? Do I need to move?"

"No, no. Stay where you are. It's just somebody I ran into at the courthouse." Carrie came through the door just then, and Frank stood to get her attention.

She smiled and walked to the table. If she was surprised to see J.J. sitting there, she didn't let on. J.J.
was the one who looked surprised. Frank quickly introduced the two of them and, feeling awkward as the
devil, helped seat her.

"A sheriff *and* a judge named Outlaw," Carrie
said. "That *is* strange."

"We've taken some ribbing from time to time,"
J.J. said, "especially since my whole name is Jesse
James Outlaw."

"And mine is Frank James Outlaw," Frank said to
her. To J.J.. he said, "I met Carrie yesterday when
she stopped by the JP's office. I went over to pack
up Horace's personal things for Ida." He turned to
Carrie and explained. "Horace died over the weekend. Ida is his wife and a second cousin to our father."

"We're kin to 'bout everybody in the county," J.J.
told her.

Carrie grinned and said to Frank, "It's a relief to
know that you're not a ghost."

"A *ghost?*" J.J. said, frowning.

"I saw him in the justice of the peace's office, and
I assumed that he was Horace Pfannepatter."

J.J. hooted with laughter. "Naw, old Horace was
bald as buckshot and had thirty years and a hundred
pounds on Frank. Are you new in town?"

Carrie shook her head. "Just visiting. I'm here doing research."

"What kind of research?" J.J. asked.

Lori returned just then with another glass of tea and
J.J.'s plate. "You folks ready to order?"

"The menu is on the blackboard," Frank told Carrie. While she read it, he ordered the spaghetti special.

"Make that two," Carrie said, glancing at J.J.'s plate. "That looks delicious."

"It is. Mary Beth makes the best chicken spaghetti in town. I'm not marrying her for her cooking, but it's a nice bonus."

"Oh," Carrie said, "are you and Mary Beth engaged?"

"Yep," J.J. said. "I'm a lucky man. What kind of research did you say you were doing?"

"Some old county records, deeds and such." She took a sip of her tea. "This is fabulous. Raspberry, isn't it?"

Frank nodded. "House specialty."

"You looking to buy some property?" J.J. asked.

What was it with J.J.? Frank wondered. He sounded like he was grilling a suspect.

Carrie chuckled. "Me? Heavens no. Please eat, J.J. Your food will get cold if you wait on us."

"Nope. Here yours is."

The waitress served plates to Carrie and Frank and added another basket of bread to the table.

B.D., one of the old guys who played dominoes and helped run the motel, passed by with a tray of food just then. B.D. greeted them all with a "hi-dee" and said, "Miss Carrie, you had a chance to talk to Millie yet?"

"Not yet."

"Millie?" J.J. asked.

"Millie down at the library," B.D. said. "Miss Carrie's one of them genealogists, don't ya know? Well, I'd better get this grub over to the office. The boys are waiting."

"You're a *genealogist?*" J.J. said.

Carrie laughed. "You make it sound like a disease."

"I think what J.J. is trying to say is that you don't look like the typical genealogist," Frank offered, trying to steer away from the interrogation. The minute the words were out of his mouth, he wanted to kick himself. *Oh, hell. Had he really said that?*

J.J. grinned like a possum in a persimmon tree. Frank turned his attention to his plate, hoping she'd ignore his gaffe. She didn't.

"And exactly what does the typical genealogist look like?" she asked, looking amused. "Have you known many?"

"Now that I think about it, I don't think I know any genealogists. You're the first."

"There's Millie," J.J. said. "She's the local expert. She's even written a book."

"I'll have to buy a copy."

She smiled, and Frank almost missed his mouth with his fork. He tried to think of something to say and drew a blank.

"What family are you researching?" J.J. asked between bites.

"I'm really not at liberty to say much about my business. Clients like to keep some things private."

J.J. laughed. "Must be a horse thief or two in the clan."

She smiled again, and the room seemed to grow brighter. "I have a couple of my own ancestors who were on the shady side. They've been expunged from the family bible. Speaking of shady characters, why in the world are you Outlaws named after outlaws?"

"It was my grandfather's idea," Frank said, relieved that finally he could contribute to the conversation. "He was a judge, too. He thought that having a memorable name would be an asset in both business and politics, so he named our father John Wesley Hardin and our uncle Butch Cassidy. I guess his idea worked. Our dad was undefeated for sheriff until he retired, and Uncle Butch was a state senator when he died."

"And now the two of you are sheriff and judge. Undefeated?"

"So far," J.J. said.

After Frank's tongue got untangled, they talked about the history of the town and the old courthouse while they ate. Carrie seemed interested and asked all kinds of questions about the town and the county. He found himself growing very comfortable talking with her.

J.J. asked, "Where's home for you, Carrie?"

"Houston."

"Our oldest brother lives in Houston," Frank told her. "He's in homicide with H.P.D."

"And his name is…"

"Cole Younger Outlaw," J.J. supplied. "And our other brother is a Texas Ranger. Sam Bass Outlaw."

"And our baby sister is with the FBI," Frank said. "Belle Starr Outlaw."

"Quite an impressive family," Carrie said.

"We try." J.J. polished off the last bite on his plate. "Now if you'll excuse me, I'm going into the kitchen to kiss the cook. Nice meeting you, Carrie." He stood, bowed slightly and left.

She smiled. "I like your brother."

"He's a good guy. Do you like his brother, too?" Frank nearly groaned. Had he really said that?

"Of course. I'm glad you didn't die."

Her attention seemed to be on his hands, and he looked down to find that he was twirling his wedding ring round and round on his finger. "Me, too. My wife did, though." *God, that was awkward.*

Carrie looked puzzled. "Did what?"

"Died. My wife was killed in a car wreck."

She reached across the table and touched his hand. "I'm so sorry. When was this?"

"It's been almost two years." He shook his head to keep the memories from intruding. "How about dessert? Mary Beth makes a mean apple tart."

"Sounds tempting, but if I eat another bite, I'll nod off over the records this afternoon. I need to scoot."

She took her wallet from her bag, but Frank waved her off. "My invitation, my treat."

"Thanks. I'll get the check next time."

"It's a deal." He stood as she said her goodbyes, then watched her walk out the door. He liked Carrie Campbell. She was warm, open and easy to talk to. Plus she was a beautiful woman.

Behind him J.J. said, "Beautiful woman."

"Is she? I hadn't noticed."

J.J. hooted. "You're lying and your feet stink!"

Frank tried to suppress a grin. "She is easy on the eyes. But don't make more out of this than it is."

"Me? I'm not making anything out of it? When are you going to see her again?"

"I don't know. Want some dessert?"

"You buying?" J.J. asked.

"I bought breakfast, you mooch."

"Say, Mary Beth and I are going over to Travis Lake Saturday night to see a musical that the college is putting on. Why don't you ask Carrie, and go with us?"

"I doubt that she'll even be here then."

"Sure she will. Mary Beth said her reservation is for several weeks. Ask her. Get out and enjoy yourself, Frank. It's time."

He took a deep breath and blew it out. "I'll think about it."

## Chapter Three

Keeping her identity secret was turning out to be a problem, Carrie thought as she hurried to her room after lunch. She'd been squirming as she'd sat there with a sheriff and a judge trying to walk a fine line between sidestepping the truth and telling a blatant lie. While she'd been very careful not to actually lie to them, neither had she said anything to correct the impression that the old man had made about her being a genealogist. In fact, she could have kissed the old codger for getting her off the hook. She hoped she wasn't getting herself into a huge mess by her evasions. It was one thing to misrepresent herself to townspeople and quite another to mislead officers of the law.

Maybe she needed to do a little genealogical research on the side to keep herself honest. Had any of her ancestors come from this area of Texas? Seems as if there might have been a great-great-uncle on her father's side whose first wife was from around here. She'd check. In the meantime, she would be wise to avoid the Outlaw brothers.

Carrie stayed so busy the rest of the day that she didn't have much time to think about him, but that evening when she took a break from studying the county platts scattered over her bed, her thoughts turned to Frank Outlaw. She lay back on her propped pillows, took a sip of her cola and remembered that smile. And the handsome contours of his face. And the timbre of his voice.

Frank Outlaw was a hunk.

And he *wasn't* married.

But she needed to forget about him. She couldn't afford to jeopardize this deal.

Easier said than done. She thought about him some more as she creamed off her makeup and put on her sleep shirt. She thought of him the next morning as she passed his office in the courthouse. And again at five of twelve when she decided to go to lunch. Not in a long, long time had she met a man that interested her as much as Frank.

*But,* she told herself, she'd be wise to steer clear of him. Basically an honest person, she felt a little guilty about giving him the wrong impression about her business in Naconiche. No. She felt a *lot* guilty.

He wasn't in the hall as he'd been the day before.

Which was good, she quickly reminded herself, if she wanted to avoid him. Maybe she'd have lunch at the City Grill. Yes. He'd be going to the tearoom.

She hurried across the street to the café. There wasn't an empty seat at the counter and all the tables were taken. Then, as she scanned the room again, their eyes met. It was Frank. If he hadn't seen her, she'd have made tracks out the door, but she didn't want to look like an idiot. She'd simply wait until there was a seat available. Trying to avoid looking at the judge, she studied the framed photographs of baseball teams hanging near the cash register.

"Carrie?"

Turning, she saw that Frank had come up behind her. She smiled. "Hello."

He smiled. "Hello. Would you like to join me?"

"Oh, I wouldn't want to intrude."

"You wouldn't be intruding. And you're not likely to find a seat anytime soon."

So much for trying to avoid him. Accepting fate, she said, "Thanks," and followed him to his table. After she was seated, she scanned the menu. "What's the special today?"

He looked amused. "Liver and onions."

She made a face and shuddered. "I hate liver and onions."

"Me, too. When my mom used to fix liver for dinner, I always offered my little brother Sam a quarter to eat mine."

"And he did it?"

"Yep. Sam would eat almost anything." He chuckled. "If the price was right."

Carrie loved that chuckle, the way it rumbled deep in his throat and sent little ripples up her spine. And his mouth fascinated her. Although it was definitely masculine, the full, curved shape of his lips was downright beautiful—and sexy as the dickens.

He must have been reading her mind, because just then the tip of his tongue appeared and moistened his lower lip. Entranced, she watched his tongue withdraw, observed his lips press together, then relax, noted the glisten left on his mouth by the action.

Darned if her toes didn't curl.

She glanced up, and his eyes locked with hers. They were dark, very dark and filled with something indefinable...but totally captivating. His eyes alone would have made him enormously attractive. Bedroom eyes they called them. The kind that made such glorious promises that women wanted to throw themselves into his arms and follow him anywhere. She wasn't immune. Her impulses ran along the same line.

"What would you like?" he asked.

A slow smile spread over her face. Wonder what he would do if she told him the truth? "What would you like?"

"I...uh—" he took a deep breath and pressed his lips together again "—think I'll have a BLT," he said to the waitress who had appeared. He closed his menu and began twirling his wedding ring.

She shrugged. "Sounds good to me." If she didn't know better, Carrie would have thought that she made the judge nervous. Why? She was tempted to ask but wise enough not to.

Her female antennae told her that he was just as attracted to her as she was to him. She'd have to be an ignoramus to have missed it. Maybe he was still mourning his wife, she reasoned. But two years was a heck of a long time.

"What was it like growing up in a large family?" Carrie asked, turning the conversation to safe territory.

"Chaotic at times, and we had our share of squabbles. But mostly it was fun. We're all very close."

They ate their sandwiches and made small talk. She carefully avoided any discussion of her work.

"Want dessert?" Frank asked. "Their cobbler isn't bad."

Carrie shook her head. "I have a yen for ice cream, and I've heard that the Double Dip has the best in town."

Frank grinned. "I can vouch for that."

"Join me?"

"Sure."

He reached for the check, but she insisted on paying. "It's my turn. You can get the ice cream."

"That's a deal. I get a family discount."

"Family?"

"My mom owns it. After she retired from teaching a few years ago, she got bored and decided to find something to do with her time. The Double Dip was up for sale, so she bought it."

They walked across the street to the old-fashioned ice-cream parlor, and as they approached, a serious wave of nostalgia rolled over Carrie. It reminded her of the little shop where Burt, one of her long line of stepfathers, used to take her when she was a kid. Was Burt number three or number four? She couldn't remember. But she had really liked him; he was a kind man and told silly jokes that made her laugh. Obviously her mother hadn't liked him nearly as well as Carrie had, for they soon packed and left, and no amount of weeping and begging had convinced her mother to stay.

A bell over the door announced their arrival. The stools at the counter were red, just like the ones from her childhood. She took a seat at the chrome-trimmed counter and inhaled the wonderful cold-sweet fragrance, a blend of smells so poignant that she could almost feel her pigtails on her shoulders.

"Gosh, this brings back memories," she said. "I love this place already. I used to go to a shop just like this one when I was a little girl."

A grandmotherly type with short gray hair bustled in from the back, drying her hands on a towel. She smiled. "Hello, son." She turned to Carrie, and Frank made the introductions.

"Carrie is in town to do some work at the courthouse, and she heard that you had the best ice cream in town," Frank said.

"I hope I can make good on that claim," Nonie Outlaw said. "What would you like?"

"Do you have peppermint?"

The woman smiled. "We surely do. It's my husband's favorite."

"Mine, too. I'll have a double dip."

"Cone or dish?"

"Oh, a cone. And do you have chocolate sprinkles?"

"Surely do."

"Put some of those on top."

When the cone was made, Carrie took the two fat scoops of peppermint ice cream, the top dark with sprinkles. She closed her eyes and savored the aroma, then licked a dollop from the side—and sighed. The taste was everything she remembered.

"I've died and gone to heaven. I can't believe that I've waited over twenty years to have another one of these. Mrs. Outlaw, this is delicious." Her tongue made another swipe, then another in a distinct pattern that was suddenly familiar.

The woman laughed. "I'm glad you like it. But most everybody just calls me Miss Nonie from my teaching days. Welcome to Naconiche. Are you going to be staying long? We have several events coming up soon that you might enjoy."

"I'll be around several weeks."

"She does genealogical research," Frank said.

"That's wonderful. Have you met Millie at the library yet?"

"Not yet, but everybody tells me she's the town authority. I plan to go by tomorrow." She turned to Frank. "Aren't you having any ice cream?"

He glanced at his watch. "I'll have to pass. I'm due back in court. Mom, put this one on my tab."

Other customers came in and Miss Nonie left to take their orders. Carrie waved goodbye to her as she and Frank left.

"This ice cream really is fabulous. I'm going to do some window-shopping while I finish it. Thanks for it and for sharing your table."

"Thanks for buying my lunch," he said.

"No problem."

He hesitated as if he wanted to say something else.

She waited, but whatever was on his mind went unsaid. He merely nodded and started across the street. A red pickup truck almost hit him. The truck driver honked and swerved, and Frank jumped back. He didn't look at her. When the way was clear, he trotted to the other side.

She wanted to call out to him, but he didn't look back.

Her ice cream started dribbling over her fingers, and she hurriedly began to lick away the mess. When she glanced up again, Frank was hurrying up the steps of the courthouse. She sighed. He even looked good from the rear. Maybe she wouldn't mind seeing a little more of the handsome Frank James Outlaw while she was in Naconiche.

FRANK FELT like such a dope. He'd nearly been creamed by that pickup. He'd been off-kilter since he'd run into Carrie in the hall outside his office. A couple of times yesterday afternoon, he'd found his mind wandering from the case he was hearing to thoughts of her. And last night he'd done more tossing and turning than sleeping, bedeviled by memories of Susan and feeling guilty as hell about being attracted to another woman.

And he *was* attracted to her. It bothered him. Bothered him so much that, trying to avoid bumping into Carrie, he'd left his office early and gone to the Grill instead of the tearoom. But it seemed that the powers that be had other ideas. When he'd looked up and seen her at the café, he'd felt a rush of elation rather than disappointment. His best efforts at trying to ignore her didn't last long. As if they had a mind of their own, his legs had gotten up and trotted in her direction.

He'd almost invited her to go to that musical in Travis Lake that J.J. had suggested. Almost. He was glad he'd kept his mouth shut. It was too soon after Susan's death to start seeing another woman. Or was it?

Sure it was. Susan had been the great love of his life. Until a couple of days ago, he had thought he'd be content to be a widower for the rest of his life. His kids, his work, that was enough for him he'd believed.

Carrie Campbell had shaken that belief. It made him nervous.

Court that afternoon was absorbing enough to hold his attention, but back in his chambers, Frank began to get that antsy feeling again and left early. When he spotted the florist across the square near his parking space, he walked over and bought a small bouquet of yellow mums tied with a white ribbon. He laid the flowers on the seat and drove to the cemetery west of town.

The wind had kicked up a little, and it rumpled his hair and flapped his tie as he walked to the familiar spot where Susan lay. Fallen leaves from an oak tree nearby made a scratching sound as they skittered across the headstone. He squatted down and brushed away leaves and a bit of grass from a recent mowing.

Hers was a simple flat marker made of a slab of pink granite with an antique brass plaque. Dogwood blossoms decorated the margin of the large plaque, and in the center was her name, Susan E. Outlaw, the dates of her birth and death, and the simple but profound message: Beloved Wife and Mother. A permanent brass vase was filled with a pretty bouquet of silk flowers that changed with the seasons, but Susan had always liked fresh flowers, so he brought them now and then.

"Hi, Suz," he whispered, laying the mums just below the marker. "I brought you some flowers. They're yellow. Your favorite color."

Now he knew that Susan wasn't there, but it was the closest he could come to physically being near her, so he often came to the cemetery to talk to her. Looking at a photograph of her or looking up at the sky or sitting in the kitchen or even in church didn't do it for him. He'd tried it. This was the last place he'd seen the body of his wife, and this was the place where he returned.

"God, Suz, I miss you so much. It's so lonely sometimes without you."

A gust of wind sent more leaves sliding across the marker.

"Did I tell you that the twins are doing really well

learning to ride their bikes? Of course they'll have training wheels for quite a while yet, so there's no need to worry about them getting bunged up.''

He told Susan everything that had been going on his life—except that he didn't mention Carrie Campbell. He couldn't quite bring himself to mention her.

Afterward he felt better. He returned to his car and headed home. This was the night he'd promised the twins they could watch the Charlie Brown special on TV.

CARRIE PUT the low-cal dinner in the small freezer compartment and the salad in the fridge. Although she'd done it hundreds of times, somehow the prospect of eating out alone that night seemed dreary, so she'd stopped by the grocery store to pick up something.

She stretched her back and rolled her head around, trying to ease the stiffness in her muscles. Exercise. That's what she needed. She'd missed jogging the past couple of days, and she felt it.

After changing hurriedly into grungies and her running shoes, she did a few warm-up exercises, then stuck her key into her pocket and went outside.

She greeted Mary Beth Parker, who was coming out of the office unit.

"Hi," Mary Beth said. "Going for a run?"

"Thought I would. What's a good route?"

"Go down this street about a quarter mile, then take a dirt road to the left. There's not much traffic there. I teach aerobics on Thursday nights in unit two. You're welcome to work out with us tomorrow if you like."

"Thanks, I'll do that."

"I was just going for a short run myself," Mary Beth said. "Mind if I join you?"

"Not at all. I'd like the company."

"I broke my foot last spring, and I still have to take it pretty easy while I'm getting back into shape. I'm not at marathon level yet."

Carrie grinned. "You don't have to worry about holding me back. A couple of miles will do it for me. Three maybe if I walk and jog."

"That's about my speed for now." They started down the road at a fast walk.

The route they took was a two-lane blacktop with pastures on one side and tall trees, mostly pines mixed with a few hardwoods, on the other. A few head of black cattle grazed in the pasture while a breeze rustled the treetops and swayed the underbrush.

"Tell me," Carrie said. "How did you come to be a chef and an innkeeper? Was it a family business?"

Mary Beth laughed. "It's a long story, and I'm no chef. I'm a cook—through necessity. And I'm not sure that running a small motel elevates me to the grand term of innkeeper. It was a family business— in a way. A distant cousin owned it, but when I inherited the Twilight Inn and the restaurant last spring, the place was a mess. Worse than a mess. The motel units had been standing vacant for years and were dilapidated beyond belief. The tearoom had been a Mexican restaurant more recently and wasn't as bad, but the roof leaked and it had mice."

"You've certainly done wonders with it, and chef or not, the food at the tearoom is great."

"Thanks. It was a lot of work, and I couldn't have done it without the help of some very good friends. I was desperate when I came back to Naconiche, and inheriting this place seemed like a godsend—until I saw the condition of it. This is where we turn."

They took the dirt road and began to jog at a slow pace. "Desperate? Sounds like an intriguing story."

As they trotted along the red dirt, Mary Beth related the tale of her return to Naconiche. She'd grown up in the town, then moved away with her parents about the time she started college. She'd met her former husband in school, married him, moved to Mississippi and lived the good life—for a while.

"Marriage to Brad wasn't the fairy tale I'd imagined it would be. Things got really bad, and we divorced. Katy and I moved into the garage apartment of a friend in Natchez.

"I was teaching aerobics, and we were getting by," Mary Beth said. "Barely. Until I injured my foot. I couldn't teach with my foot in a cast, and I was almost broke when I discovered that I'd inherited the Twilight Inn. I thought we were saved."

"Except that it wasn't what you expected."

"Lord no. It was a disaster." Mary Beth laughed. "Katy and I lived in the restaurant for a while."

"In the *restaurant?*"

Mary Beth grinned. "Yes. It wasn't so bad until it rained and the roof leaked like a sieve. J.J. came to the rescue. This is where we turn around."

They started back to the motel, walking for a while, then resuming their jog. "Your fiancé seems like a really nice guy."

"He is. Sometimes I think that probably I should have stayed in Naconiche and married him to begin with. But I know we were too young in those days."

"So you knew him before?"

Mary Beth nodded. "He was my first love. We dated a long time."

"And he never married?"

"Nope. Says he was pining for me all that time. And if you believe that, I've got this bridge…"

They both laughed.

"And you're not married or committed to some special fella?" Mary Beth asked.

"Never have been. Never will be." Her tone was sharper than she meant it to be.

Mary Beth was quiet for a long time. The only sounds were their breathing and the slap of their soles on the road, but Carrie could almost hear the wheels going around as her running partner considered possible explanations for her statement—and was too polite to question her further. Carrie should have kept her mouth shut. She'd never been prone to sharing intimacies with anyone, but she'd felt drawn to Mary Beth almost immediately and felt very comfortable with her—almost as if they'd been friends for a long time. And God knows, Mary Beth had certainly been candid about her life.

After about a half mile, Carrie chuckled and said lightly, "I always figured that my mother was married enough for the both of us. Seven times at last count."

"*Seven?* You're kidding."

"Nope."

"Is she still living?"

"Alive and well and in the south of France. The last couple of times, she married Europeans."

"Do you see her often?"

"Only occasionally. We don't have much in common. My mother is a dependent type who must have a man to take care of her. I don't need anybody to take care of me. And the truth is, my work keeps me on the road too much for a long-term relationship. Men seem to want their women around for more than a week here and there. Or at least that's been my experience."

"I suppose that's true. And you travel all the time doing genealogical research?"

"That and various other kinds of specialized research. I stay pretty busy. Where's your daughter tonight?"

"J.J. took Katy over to Frank's house to watch a special TV program with his twins."

"His *twins?* Frank has twins?"

"A boy and a girl Katy's age. They're all in kindergarten together."

Carrie was stunned. She'd never thought about his having children, though it made sense when you considered he was a widower. That put the cap on it for sure. So much for Frank. While she'd never really considered any kind of serious relationship between them, even the remote possibility of a few casual dates while she was in town had disappeared. From now on she'd avoid him like the plague.

Men with children were invariably looking for a mother for their kids, and that wasn't for her. She didn't know a thing about kids and certainly wasn't cut out to be a mother. She'd had a lousy role model.

# Chapter Four

Her resolve didn't last long. Carrie ran into Frank as she was coming out of the assessor's office at a quarter to twelve, and darned if her heart didn't skip a beat.

"Hello," he said, closing his door behind him. "Going to lunch?"

"Yes, at the tearoom." She wasn't going to eat at cholesterol city across the square just to avoid Frank Outlaw.

He smiled. "Me, too. Want a ride?"

"Uh, no. I need to do some work in my room afterward. I'll take my car," she said.

"Mind if I hitch a ride with you? I'll get Dad to drop me back here."

"No problem. You joining your father today?" she asked.

"He and J.J. and I usually eat together on Thursdays. That's chocolate cake day. We're all suckers for Mary Beth's chocolate cake."

"I'm a sucker for anything chocolate."

"I'll have to remember that."

He grinned. Why did he have to grin? He looked so darned sexy when he grinned. And why did he have to put his hand to her back when they walked to her car? Didn't he know that it made funny prickles zip up and down her spine like a Japanese express train? Her resolve to cool her feelings for Frank was dissolving fast.

Since the first time she'd seen him, he'd had a singular effect on her, and it seemed to have grown instead of diminished. What was it about this particular man that shot her defenses? He had two arms, two legs and all the rest of the body parts typical of the male gender—and she'd never melted like ice cream in a skillet over other guys. At least not since she'd been sixteen and ape over Jon Bon Jovi.

As they drove away from the courthouse Frank ran his hand over the leather seat, and his fingertips brushed her leg. The touch hit her like a jolt of electricity. Did he do that on purpose? She glanced at him, but his hands were clamped together, and he was engrossed in studying the dash.

He looked up and said, "Nice car."

"Thanks. I like it."

"You must be a very good genealogist."

She smiled. "I am. I'm good at all kinds of research that I do, but the car was a thirtieth birthday gift from my mother and her husband." She didn't add that her mother had told her latest catch that it was her daughter's twenty-first birthday. Hence the special gift. After her face-lift, Amanda had shaved nine years off her age, so she'd shaved nine years off Carrie's age as well. One thing she'd have to say for her mother, she'd made out like a bandit in her last couple of trips down the aisle. Amanda had plenty stashed away for her golden years.

"Her husband? Not your father?" Frank asked.

"No. My father died in an accident when I was only two. Amanda, my mother, has been married several times. I believe the latest one is a retired investor. He's French. Jacques something-or-the-other. We've never met."

"I take it that you and your mother aren't close," he said quietly.

She glanced over and saw sincere compassion in his eyes, and tears suddenly sprang into her own. Damn. She never cried. And certainly not over Amanda. Long ago she'd learned that the only thing crying accomplished was to make her face blotchy. That was another thing about Frank. He seemed to be able to fly under the radar of her emotional control.

She took a deep breath. "Not really. I never seemed to fit in with her plans."

"That's tough on kids."

"I survived. Mary Beth tells me that you have twins."

"I do. Janey and Jimmy. They're five."

She couldn't think of anything else to say. She knew zilch about children. And, she reminded herself, she really didn't want to encourage any further intimacy. She'd said too much already. Carrie clamped her teeth together and tried not to squirm.

The silence dragged on for an eternity.

Finally Frank said, "You mentioned doing other kinds of research besides genealogy."

"Yes."

"What kinds?"

Choosing her words carefully, she said, "Titles, missing heirs, that sort of thing." Which was technically true.

"Ah. Missing heirs. Sounds intriguing. Found any

folks in Naconiche County who have inherited a bundle from a long-lost relative?''

She laughed. ''Not yet.''

''I think everybody has had the dream that some long-lost relative rolling in dough will kick the bucket and leave a fortune to them.''

''Do you have any long-lost relatives?''

''Only my mother's great-uncle Heck Tatum. He went to California and was never heard from again.''

''When was this?'' Carrie asked.

''I'm not exactly sure. Sometime before 1920, I believe.''

''You never know. He may have struck it rich in real estate.''

Frank chuckled. ''I doubt it. From what my mother tells me about Uncle Heck, it's more likely that he wound up in jail than in the money. He was the black sheep of his family. I think he left here just one step ahead of the sheriff.''

When they arrived at the tearoom, Carrie meant to duck out and go to her room for a few minutes, but she was so intrigued by the tale of Frank's errant relative that she forgot her plan and walked with him to the door.

''What did he do?'' she asked.

''You mean, to get the sheriff after him? As I recall the story, I believe that Uncle Heck made his living cooking moonshine and stealing cows. Folks around here don't cotton to cattle rustling. Back then it was sometimes a hanging offense.''

*''Hanging?''*

''Yep.''

A few people were waiting for tables, but Frank

waved to someone. "There are Dad and J.J. Come on, we'll join them."

"Oh, I don't want to horn in when you're having lunch with your family."

"You wouldn't be horning in. Come on."

He steered her to the table for four.

J.J. and the older man stood as they approached, and Frank introduced Carrie to his father. Wes Outlaw was tall like his sons and she could see the family resemblance except that his dark hair was gray, his fingers were knobby and his waist had thickened a bit. He had the same great smile, and it flashed across his weathered face when he told her to call him Wes.

"I was just telling Carrie about Mama's great-uncle Heck."

"Ah, the cattle rustler," Wes said.

"And the moonshiner," Carrie added.

Wes grinned. "Nobody around here was bothered much by the moonshining—fact is, most folks bought a jug from him now and then, I understand. But stealing cows is serious business."

All three of the Outlaws were raconteurs, and they kept her entertained during lunch with funny stories about some of the lawless characters in the county's history. They seemed to enjoy topping one another's yarns.

As they lingered over coffee and dessert, Carrie laughed as J.J. told in great detail about the night that a young man and his friends had a few too many beers and put a pig in the mayor's Cadillac. "That pig made a *big* mess," J.J. said.

"It *didn't*," Carrie said, laughing.

J.J. grinned. "It did. All over everywhere."

"I had a hard time," Frank said, "keeping a

straight face when those kids were brought before me.''

''What did you do to them?''

''Gave them a stern lecture and made them put in a lot of hours of community service.''

Carrie glanced at her watch, then looked around the room. The place was almost deserted. ''Sorry, but I have to go.'' She reached for her wallet.

''Today's on me,'' Frank said.

''I'll get the next one.'' Why had she said that? What happened to the resolution that she wasn't going to spend any more time with Frank Outlaw? She mentally shrugged. What was the harm? She enjoyed his company; she liked his family. No big deal. In a few weeks she'd be in West Texas or Oklahoma on her next project. She was going to take a page from Amanda's book and live for the moment.

She said her goodbyes and went to her room to work.

''MIND IF I CATCH a ride back to the courthouse with one of you?'' Frank asked over a second cup of coffee.

''Be glad to drop you off,'' his father said. ''Say, I like your young woman. Seems to have a head on her shoulders.''

''She's not *my* young woman,'' Frank told him. ''She's just someone in town for a few days to do some research.''

''What kind of research?''

''Genealogy,'' J.J. said.

''And titles and missing heirs,'' Frank added.

''Hmm,'' Wes said, rubbing his mouth the way he

always did when he was thinking. "What kind of titles?"

"Land, I imagine. She spends a lot of time in the
tax office."

"Did you invite her to go with us to the musical
Saturday night?" J.J. asked Frank.

"Uh, no."

"Why the hell not? She's single, good-looking and
fun to talk to. Ask her."

"I'll think about it."

J.J. gave an exasperated snort. "I'm going to the
kitchen to see Mary Beth."

Wes pushed back his chair. "You 'bout ready to
go?"

"Anytime. Just don't you start on me."

"Start on you? About what, son?"

"About Carrie."

His dad held up his hands in surrender. "I won't
say a word."

CARRIE WORKED in her room for the entire afternoon.
There were some serious gaps in the information
she'd gathered so far. She was going to have to run
down some deeds, land titles *and* some missing heirs.
She hadn't lied about that to Frank. One of the tough
things about her job was locating heirs when property
owners died and didn't leave a will. Texas had very
specific guidelines about who inherited in such cases.
Figuring out who owned what could get complicated.

This part of her job required patience and persis-
tence. It was often easier simply to talk to the existing
landowners and get information to at least point her
in the right direction, but since Uncle Tuck wanted
things kept quiet as long as possible, she was handi-

capped in her search. If she ran into too many problems, she'd have to start questioning the locals. Maybe that's where Millie the librarian might help.

After working at her computer for several hours, Carrie felt as if she was going cross-eyed. She saved her work, then stretched and got up. No wonder her eyes were tired. It was growing dark. But at least her material was organized, and she was ready to start work at the county clerk's office the next day.

She thought about jogging, then remembered that this was the night Mary Beth taught aerobics. She ate an apple, washed her face, then changed into her sneakers and workout clothes.

By the time Carrie arrived at unit two, several women had gathered.

Mary Beth looked up and saw her. "Hi, Carrie. Come on in and let me get you acquainted with everybody."

She led her to two women and introduced her to Ellen, a blonde who was in real estate, and Dixie, a brunette who was in remarkably good shape for a mother of six children. Mary Beth said, "These two are my best buddies from high school. Can you believe that we used to be cheerleaders together?"

Carrie laughed. "I was a high school cheerleader, too. It seems like eons ago."

She also met Dr. Kelly Martin, a stunning green-eyed redhead, whose long curls were held atop her head with a big yellow clip.

"Dr. Kelly is the person you want to see if you break your leg or get the flu," Mary Beth said. "The best doctor in Naconiche."

Dr. Kelly grinned and stuck out her hand. "Hi,

Carrie. I hope you don't need to see me professionally. Are you new in town?''

"No, just visiting for a few weeks." Carrie studied
the doctor's face. "You look very familiar to me.
Have we met?"

"I don't know. I was just thinking the same thing.
I grew up in Dallas. Did you?"

Carrie shook her head. "Did you go to the Uni-
versity of Texas?"

"Sure did." She smiled knowingly, then mentioned the name of a sorority.

Memories flashed through Carrie's mind, and she
smiled as well. "Kelly Martin. Now I remember. You
were a year or two ahead of me. But your hair was
long and straight then, and you wore glasses."

"I've had Lasik on my eyes, and I don't have time
anymore to blow-dry this mop into submission every
morning. It's great to see you again. You look gorgeous as always. It's those eyes I remembered."
Kelly turned to Mary Beth. "Would you believe that
Carrie and I were sorority sisters at UT years ago?"

"You're kidding! That's wonderful."

"Are you going to be in town over the weekend?"
Kelly asked Carrie.

"Sure am."

"Fantastic. Let's get together Sunday afternoon
and catch up."

They made plans for a late lunch, and there was
barely time for a brief exchange of names with four
other women before the class began. One of them was
named Millie. The librarian? Carrie wondered.

She didn't wonder long because Mary Beth went
into her drill sergeant mode, and for almost an hour
Carrie was too busy keeping the pace to think about

much of anything. By the time they stopped to cool down, she was pooped and wet with sweat. She stretched out on the floor, flung her arms wide and sucked in deep breaths. "I may die," she said to Kelly, who was next to her.

Kelly laughed. "I doubt it. But Mary Beth's no wuss. She's tough. I've got to run home and shower and make rounds at the hospital. See you Sunday."

Carrie wiggled her fingers. After several of the women had left, she rose. "I thought I was in better shape," she said to Mary Beth, who was standing with Ellen and Dixie.

"You're in better shape than me," Ellen said. "I still can't make it through the whole session without resting several times."

"Me, either," Dixie chimed in.

"Yeah," Ellen said, "but you had a baby not too long ago."

"You're all doing great," Mary Beth said. "Remember that I said you should go at your own pace. You should have taken a break, Carrie."

She chuckled. "What can I tell you? I'm a high achiever. I'm going to drag myself to my room and take a shower."

"Have you had dinner?" Mary Beth asked.

"No, but I picked up something to nuke later."

"Why don't you join Ellen, Dixie and me at the tearoom for a light supper? It's only leftovers, but we'd love to have you."

Carrie laughed. "I'm a bit odoriferous for a social occasion."

"Oh, piddle," Dixie said with a dismissing wave. "We've all been sweating like pigs. Forget about it and come on. Mary Beth has saved us some chocolate cake.''

''Chocolate? How can I resist? That stuff is sinful.''

The four of them trudged over to the tearoom. Or rather, three of them trudged. Mary Beth still had a spring in her step.

They spent a leisurely hour over their simple meal, and Carrie thoroughly enjoyed getting to know the women, making girl-talk. Her job kept her on the road so much that she didn't have much time to spend with friends, especially female friends. In fact, now that she thought about it, she didn't have very many women friends left. Their lives had taken them in different directions, and she hadn't taken the time to cultivate new friendships to fill the void.

Dixie was the first to rise. ''I've got to get a move on or Jack will be sending out a posse,'' she said. ''Great to meet you, Carrie. I hope you'll join us for as long as you're in town.''

''Me, too,'' Ellen said. ''Nobody will be sending out a posse for me, but I know my sitter would like to get home early, and I'm riding with Dixie.''

After the two left, Carrie helped carry the dishes into the kitchen. ''This was really fun,'' she said. ''Thanks for inviting me.''

''We enjoyed having you,'' Mary Beth said. ''Listen, if you're going to be around tomorrow night and don't have plans, why don't you go to the football game with us? Then, watching high school football may not be your idea of a scintillating evening.''

''Lord, I haven't been to a football game in ages.''

''We have a winning team this year, and everybody in town will be there. It's the only Friday night entertainment around here. Go with us. We'll have hot dogs and peanuts, and root for the Mustangs.''

"With you and Dixie and Ellen?''

"No, with J.J., Katy and me. I insist. Be ready about six-thirty. Wear jeans and bring a jacket.''

Carrie tried to weasel out of the invitation, but Mary Beth wouldn't take no for an answer.

What the heck. She didn't have anything better to do, and sitting around a hotel room alone with only a TV for company got very old very quickly.

"You're on,'' Carrie said. "Shall I bring my pom-poms?''

## Chapter Five

J.J. walked ahead and carried Katy while Mary Beth and Carrie brought along the stadium seats. As they moved with the crowd to the bleachers, smells of popcorn, peanuts and fall in the air brought a wave of sweet nostalgia. The band was playing, and the team ran around the field warming up. Excitement was in the air, and it was catching. Carrie felt a zing run through her, and a grin spread over her face.

"This brings back a lot of memories," Carrie said.

"Doesn't it? Where did you go to high school?"

"Cypress-Fairbanks. It's a suburb of Houston. Those were some of the happiest days of my life."

But those days hadn't started out happy, she recalled. Carrie had felt alone and abandoned when her mother had dumped her with Uncle Tuck when Carrie was barely fourteen. Amanda's soon-to-be husband was a mining engineer.

"Darling," Amanda had told her, "Richard and I will be traveling to all sorts of remote places, and I want you to have proper schooling. They have wonderful schools in Cy-Fair, and you'll get a good background for college. It breaks my heart to leave you, but I'll visit often."

She hadn't. Despite the teary-eyed hugs and kisses and promises, Amanda hadn't shown up for two years. With Amanda, out of sight was out of mind. Carrie always suspected that one of the reasons her mother had ditched her was that Richard didn't want a teenager around.

Tucker Campbell, her father's older brother, was an independent oilman and a widower with a sixteen-year-old son, Sam. Uncle Tuck didn't know what to do with a teenage girl, either, but he had a heart as big as Texas and was game to try. She adored Sam and Uncle Tuck and loved living on the ranch with a horse of her own and making new friends at the high school where Sam paved the way for her.

Her school's stadium, the one where she'd cheered her football player cousin, was very much like this one, she thought as she followed J.J. and Mary Beth up the stairs.

When they reached a spot on the fifty-yard line about halfway up the bleachers, J.J. said, "Here we are, Katy-bug," and put the child down. "You're going to have to go on a diet. You're getting heavy."

Katy giggled. "You always say that."

"I do? I'll have to think up a new line." He smiled and tapped her nose gently. "And you're not fat. You're just right."

The little girl beamed. "I want a hot dog."

"Already?" J.J. asked as he set up the stadium seats on the weathered wood bleachers.

Katy nodded and took a seat between Mary Beth and J.J. Carrie sat on the end next to Mary Beth.

"Let me catch my breath," J.J. said, "and I'll do a concession run. What do you ladies want?"

He took orders for hot dogs, drinks, popcorn and peanuts.

"How are you going to carry all that?" Carrie asked. "Want me to go and help?"

"Naw, I'm resourceful. I can handle it."

"It's a man thing," Mary Beth said as his boots clattered down the wooden steps.

Carrie smiled. "I understand macho." And she did. From the time she was fourteen, she'd learned how to navigate in a male world. That background had served her well in her studies and her work.

Mary Beth waved at someone and Carrie turned to look. Frank was making his way toward them with a pair of dark-haired children about Katy's size. His twins, she surmised. This was the first time she'd seen him in anything other than business clothes. He had on well-worn jeans and a plaid western shirt under his jean jacket. He wore black boots and a black cowboy hat that looked to be the twin of the one J.J. always wore. And he looked darned good in his cowboy duds.

Darned good.

"Well, hello," he said to her, smiling broadly. "I'm surprised to see you here."

"And I'm surprised to see you, Judge."

"Our family has season tickets for this whole row. Have had for years. We're all big Mustang fans." He took three stadium seats from a large canvas bag he carried and started setting them up. "Carrie, this is my daughter Janey and my son Jimmy. Kids, say hello to Miss Carrie."

They both said a shy hello, then Janey tugged on Frank's pant leg and whispered, "I want to sit by Katy."

"Do you mind?" Frank asked Carrie.

"Not at all." Carrie rose to change seats and by the time the kids had shuffled everybody around to accommodate them, Carrie ended up sitting between Janey and Frank.

"Thanks. They're bosom buddies," Frank said, nodding to the two whispering, giggling girls.

"Dad," Jimmy said, "I'm hungry. Can I have a hot dog?"

"You're always hungry," Frank said, ruffling his son's hair. "Excuse me," he said to Carrie. "Old tradition. Would you like a hot dog or a soft drink?"

"Thanks, but J.J.'s already gone to get ours."

"Be right back."

Frank and Jimmy left, and Carrie turned her attention to the field where the cheerleaders were gathering, remembering the times when she'd done the same thing. She felt a small hand on her thigh and glanced down at the child sitting beside her.

Janey was staring up at her, unblinking. "You have very pretty eyes."

Carrie smiled. "Thank you. So do you." And she did. The child's eyes were a carbon copy of her dad's intense dark ones.

"But mine are only brown. Yours are the color of my very favorite dress. I'm five. How old are you?"

"I'm thirty."

"That's very, very old, but not as old as a hundred. I can count to a hundred. Want to hear me?"

Carrie was stuck. She wasn't excited by the prospect, but what could she say? "Sure."

"You want the long count or the short count?"

"How about the short count?"

"Ten, twenty, thirty, fifty, seventy…forty, ninety, a hundred." Janey smiled broadly.

"Excellent," Carrie said, returning the smile.

Janey absolutely beamed.

"You left out sixty," Katy piped up.

"When I get big, I'm going to be a cheerleader like Rachel," Janey said. "That's Rachel." She pointed to the group of girls waiting to lead the team onto the field.

"I was a cheerleader when I was in high school," Carrie said.

Janey's eyes grew big. "You were?"

"My mommy was a cheerleader, too," Katy said. "And she was a queen and rode around the square."

"My mommy did, too." Janey turned to Carrie and added, "My mommy is in heaven with God's angels. A drunk driver killed her in her car."

Carrie sure didn't know how to respond to that one, but she needn't have worried. The girls started whispering and giggling between themselves again and no response was needed.

The guys soon returned with cardboard trays full of drinks and plastic sacks hanging from their arms.

"I'm glad we made it back before the kickoff," J.J. said. "That place down there is a zoo." He and Frank distributed food and drinks to everybody just as the teams lined up to begin.

Carrie felt another poke on her thigh and glanced to Janey.

"You're supposed to stand up for kickoff, Miss Carrie," Janey whispered. "Would you please lift me up so I won't spill my root beer?"

She noticed that Mary Beth was helping Katy stand in her seat, so Carrie hoisted Janey in the same way.

"Thank you," Janey whispered. Then she thrust one arm in the air and screamed at the top of her lungs, "Go Mustangs!"

"She plans to be a cheerleader," Frank said, grinning.

"She'll be a good one," Carrie said, playfully unstopping her ears with her index fingers.

"There's Alan," Jimmy yelled, waving at a towheaded boy across the aisle and two rows up. "Can Alan sit with us, Daddy?"

"Sure, there's plenty of room."

A drumroll started from the band and a hum from the pep squad. The opposing team was in blue shirts and the home team in white. White was receiving. After the kickoff, a little guy caught the ball at the ten-yard line, tore down the field and danced his way almost to the fifty. The crowd went wild.

Before she finished her hot dog, the Mustangs scored. She found herself getting as excited as everybody around her.

Soon they had finished the hot dogs and had started on popcorn and peanuts. Carrie felt a familiar poking on her thigh.

"Miss Carrie, will you open this for me?" Janey thrust out a peanut.

"Sure." She took the peanut, cracked the shell and offered the nuts to Janey.

"Thank you. You see that man who's throwing the ball? He's the quarterback. My daddy was a quarterback."

"My daddy was a quarterback, too," Katy said.

"He was not," Janey said. "You don't have a daddy."

"I do, too. He's in the pokey."

Carrie glanced at Mary Beth, who only shrugged and smiled mysteriously. "It's a long story," she said. "Katy, I've told you that's not a nice word."

"J.J., were you a quarter?" Katy asked.

"A quarter?"

"A quarterback," Janey corrected. "But he can't be a quarterback because my daddy was a quarterback."

"I sure was," J.J. said. "Your daddy is older than I am, Janey. He just kept the place warm 'til I got there."

Frank snorted. "In your dreams, runt. Who led the team to the state playoffs?"

"And who lost the finals?" J.J. retorted with a playful smirk.

"No comment."

Carrie shelled another peanut for Janey, then turned to Frank. "So you were a football player?"

"Every boy who grows up in Naconiche plays football. Even a few of the girls try out."

"Any of them ever make it?"

"We had a girl kicker a couple of years ago. She was darned good. She was the sister of that kid who put the pig in the mayor's car."

"Did you play in college?"

He shook his head. "I banged up my knee in that final playoff game. Which was just as well."

"Why is that?"

"I wasn't good enough to play at one of the prestigious schools, and if I'd gotten a football scholarship at some little Podunk college somewhere, I wouldn't have gotten as good an education as I did at UT."

"You went to UT? So did I."

When they compared years, they found that he had

started law school when she was a freshman. She almost mentioned that she went to UT law school as well, then decided not to open that can of worms.

The Mustangs scored again, and everybody jumped up and yelled.

At halftime the band performed, and Carrie was impressed with its precision. Katy and Janey were impressed with the twirlers.

"I'm going to be a twirler when I get big," Janey said to Carrie. "And I'm going to play the flute like Beverly. That's Beverly right there on the front row. Her brother is in my class. His name is Zack. Where's Daddy?"

"He took Jimmy to the bathroom," Carrie told her. "Remember?"

"Oh, yeah. Me and Katy went earlier. To miss the crowd."

Soon after the second half started, the opponents scored, then the Mustangs kicked a field goal. The visiting team began a slow march down the field while the Mustangs fans shouted with the cheerleaders, "Defense! Defense! Push 'em back. Push 'em back. Hold 'em! Hold 'em!"

Carrie was amused when she found herself yelling along with the crowd, but she'd gotten into the spirit of the game and old habits had surfaced.

"You having a good time?" Frank asked.

"I really am. I'd forgotten how much I like football. I may be hoarse tomorrow."

"Are you staying in town for the weekend?"

"Yes. I have plenty to keep me busy."

"J.J. and Mary Beth are going to a college musical in Travis Lake tomorrow night. Would you like to join them with me? We'll have dinner first."

Before she even thought it through, Carrie said, "Sure."

He smiled. "Great. We'll pick you up about six."

Carrie felt something in her lap and looked down. Janey's head nestled there. She was sound asleep. The strangest sensation went over Carrie, and she found herself smiling as she gently brushed the child's dark hair back from her forehead.

"Looks like I'd better take these two home," Frank said, noticing his daughter. "Jimmy is getting droopy-eyed, too."

He reached over to gather up his daughter. His arm brushed against her breasts, and his hands rubbed against her lap as he shifted and lifted the child. Carrie was exceedingly aware of each movement, though she tried her best to act casual about the process. Still, her breasts tingled and her thighs felt as if he'd caressed them.

*Stop it!* she told herself, irritated by her reaction. Was she so hard up that she was getting all excited about something so simple and innocent? But it seemed to take an eternity for him to get hold of Janey and take her into his arms. And during that eternity, his arms and hands seemed to fondle very intimate areas of Carrie's body. Or was it simply her imagination?

She didn't dare look at him. She glanced at Mary Beth. Mary Beth was watching Frank struggle with Janey.

"Katy's getting sleepy, too," Mary Beth said. "And the Mustangs are way ahead. Mind if we leave pretty soon?"

"Not at all," Carrie replied. "Anytime." She

waved to Frank as he rose carrying Janey with one arm and leading Jimmy with the other hand.

Soon Katy climbed into J.J.'s lap and put her head on his shoulder, so they decided to call it a night as well.

"The kids love coming to games," Mary Beth told Carrie as they walked to the car, "but they rarely make it to the end."

"This was fun," Carrie said. "Thanks for asking me."

On the trip back to the motel and even while she dressed for bed, Carrie could still feel the zing in her body from the adrenaline she'd generated at the game. Or was some of that zing caused by Frank Outlaw?

Honestly? Maybe a little of both.

And honestly, she was looking forward to going out with him on Saturday night. She hadn't had a date with an interesting, good-looking man in…well, she couldn't remember the last decent date she'd had.

SATURDAY MORNING Carrie spent an hour sorting and resorting her wardrobe and couldn't find a thing that she thought was suitable for that night. Mary Beth had said that it wouldn't be a fancy evening, but Carrie didn't seem to have just the right thing. Everything seemed either too casual or too businesslike. This was a good opportunity to visit that neat boutique on the square.

In no time, she'd found three outfits that she couldn't decide among. One was an amethyst dress with a fabulous matching sweater that had tone on tone embroidered designs. Another was a simple black dress that looked great with either a Chanel-style black jacket or a shirt jacket in paisley. Or there was the dressy pants outfit in a luscious shade of deep teal with a sexy camisole and a long, loose top that felt heavenly.

It was impossible to decide. So she bought all three plus the extra jacket and a new pair of dressy black slacks. She could mix and match and be ready for all occasions.

She didn't feel at all guilty spending so much money. Her job paid very well; she was on an expense account; her car was paid for; her Houston town house was furnished beautifully—not that she ever got to spend much time there. In fact, she decided to buy some new shoes and lingerie as well. It felt great to splurge.

After she stowed all the packages in her trunk, she wandered down to the ice-cream shop for a double dip cone. With sprinkles.

Carrie had a nice visit with Miss Nonie while she ate her treat, then she drove around a few back roads getting a bead on some of the properties she would start negotiating on in two or three weeks. She had focused on the critical core first. Next week she'd start researching the adjoining properties, which would be part of the second unit Uncle Tuck wanted.

By midafternoon she had returned to her room to bathe and wash her hair. She still hadn't decided which of the outfits to wear. She felt a bit like a girl getting ready for her first prom. How silly, she told herself. But the butterflies in her stomach didn't listen.

She finally gave up and called Mary Beth to ask what she was wearing.

"A kind of semi-dressy red pants outfit," Mary Beth said. "But anything is okay. Really. Oh, I wouldn't wear jeans or a black cocktail dress, but anywhere in between is fine.''

The black she'd bought wasn't a cocktail dress, but Carrie decided it was too…somber. The amethyst? Maybe. The clerk had raved and said it was stunning with her eyes. But the teal pants outfit was a safe bet. It was very flattering and it felt great. Mary Beth was wearing pants; she'd wear pants.

She changed her mind a dozen times before she finished her makeup. Finally, she muttered, ''Oh, hell, Carrie. It's not world peace.'' Grabbing the teal pants, she pulled them on.

She was dressed and ready forty-five minutes early.

Disgusted with herself, she pulled off the pants and jacket, laying them neatly on the bed so they wouldn't wrinkle and turned on her computer to do some work.

When there was a knock at the door sometime later, she glanced at her watch and was horrified to find that it was six o'clock and she was wearing only a camisole and panty hose.

''Just a minute!'' she yelled, running to the door to peek out the spyhole.

Frank stood outside wearing a dark sport coat and looking good enough to eat with a spoon.

''Give me just a sec!'' she called before she darted back to the bed for her clothes.

On the way she ran into the corner of the bed frame, banged up her shin and popped a hole in her hose. Faster than a Daytona race car, a huge run zipped down her leg. With every step, the run widened and slithered lower until it extended to her toes in a ragged nylon ladder.

She had to change her panty hose quickly. Ripping

off the damaged ones, she grabbed another new pair. The package seemed hermetically sealed.

After much fumbling and muttering, she got them out and started putting them on, but she got one leg twisted wrong and felt as if her left thigh was in a vise. Stripping off the twisted leg, she straightened it and started over.

By that time she was sweating, and the blasted things wouldn't slide on properly. The crotch was around her knees.

''To hell with it!''

She threw the second pair on the floor and yanked on her pants. After a quick blot of her damp face, she fanned furiously with a sheaf of papers from her desk. She pulled on her jacket and crammed her bare feet into her new shoes. The shoes didn't fit as well as they should, but she didn't want to take time to dust her feet with powder.

Quickly, she turned off her computer and made a last check in the mirror. She picked up her purse, took two deep breaths and hurried to open the door.

## Chapter Six

Frank was getting more nervous by the second. It had taken him half an hour to decide which of his new silk ties to wear, then he'd arrived early and had to drive around for ten minutes to kill time.

When Carrie opened the door, his heart almost stopped. She looked gorgeous, and a damp, perfumed woman-scent wafted from the room with her, intimate and tantalizing. His gaze traveled from her sexy high heels to her mouth—and stopped there, transfixed.

"Hi," she said, smiling.

Was it his imagination or did her lips seem more lush, more provocative? A powerful urge prodded him to take her into his arms and kiss her. Instead, he returned the smile. "Hi, yourself. You look lovely. Am I too early?"

"Thanks, and no. I was working and lost track of the time."

He led her to his car and helped her in. When they were about to pull away she suddenly looked startled. "Something wrong?" he asked

"Uh…no. Nothing. Nothing at all. Where are Mary Beth and J.J.?"

"Mary Beth had some business in Travis Lake, so

they went ahead. We're going to meet them at the restaurant. Do you mind?''

''No, of course not.''

As they drove, the silence hung heavy in the car. Frank tried to think of something to say and drew a blank. The only thing on his mind was the intoxicating scent of her that filled the car and the lushness of her lips. Fact was, he'd had a wild dream about her the night before that had stayed in his head all day. A hot and heavy erotic dream. Just remembering it got him worked up…and feeling guilty as hell.

He could try to deny it from now till the Fourth of July, but there was a powerful chemistry between Carrie and him, and tonight it seemed even more potent. The connection was almost palpable, and he'd never experienced anything quite like it. She must have felt it, too, for she squirmed restlessly a time or two and flashed him a knowing smile that telegraphed a message straight to his primal male instincts.

He'd glanced back at the road just in time to keep from rear-ending a semi. It shook him.

Frank was itching to get his hands on Carrie, but if he didn't get his mind off having her in bed, he'd run them into a ditch.

Finally he managed to say, ''How is your work going?''

She hesitated for several seconds, then said. ''Fine.''

''Have you met Millie from the library yet?''

''I met her at aerobics class the other night. I also ran into an old sorority sister. Kelly Martin.''

Her mention of Kelly started them talking about old college days and hangouts in Austin, and their conversation grew easy and relaxed for the rest of the half-hour trip. It helped keep his mind off his libido and the car safely on the road.

CARRIE THOROUGHLY enjoyed the seafood and the company at the upscale restaurant where they'd met J.J. and Mary Beth. The place was tucked into a corner of a cobbled plaza filled with interesting small shops. That is, she enjoyed herself after she became somewhat accustomed to the fact that she wasn't wearing any panties.

After the disasters with her panty hose, and in her rush to dress, she'd forgotten to put on panties before she'd yanked on the pants to her outfit. She hadn't realized her omission until she'd slid into the front seat of Frank's car. He'd obviously noticed her stunned expression, but she'd tried to cover her reaction when he questioned her. She'd considered running back to her room, then dismissed the idea. It was her secret, and it would be a kick—once she adjusted to the sensation.

The fluid fabric felt very strange against her bare skin, very…decadent. Of course she'd heard of women deliberately going on dates without underwear as a turn-on, but she'd never tried it. It worked. She felt a little naughty. And damned sexy.

In the car coming over, she'd had the greatest urge to throw off her seat belt and jump Frank's bones. Sexual energy shot around in that car like ricocheting bullets. He must have felt it because he'd looked at her a couple of times like he wanted to pull off onto a dark road.

But he was a *judge* for goshsakes. And a *father*.

And one heck of a hunk. She itched to rip off his

tie, unbutton his shirt and run her fingers over his chest. Was it hairy? she wondered.

Carrie glanced at Frank as she spooned a bite of chocolate mousse into her mouth. He winked at her. And darned if she didn't feel her face grow warm. Surely he couldn't read her mind.

"Mary Beth," J.J. said. "What's the name of that musical we're going to see? I forgot."

"*Music Man.* I think Barry Bledsoe is going to play the lead." To Carrie, she said, "He's dean of the fine arts department and performed in New York in his younger days. I understand he's great."

When the check came, Frank glanced at his watch and said, "Looks like we have some extra time before the performance. Want another cup of coffee?"

"Let's go peek in some of the stores outside," Mary Beth said.

So, with a few minutes to spare before the show, they walked around the cobbled plaza and window-shopped.

That was a mistake.

Carrie's right shoe was uncomfortable, but her left shoe began dealing her misery. Her little toe felt as if it were in a vise, and the ball of her foot pinched and burned like the dickens. Wearing brand-new high heels, especially without stockings, had been stupid.

By the time they drove to the college and walked from the parking lot to the theater, she had to fight to keep from limping. She could feel blisters rising the size of silver dollars.

They found their seats and sat with the women in the middle and the men on each end. There was barely a moment to glance through the program before the lights dimmed.

Good. At last she could slip out of those blasted shoes.

*Ah.* She wiggled her toes. *Heaven.* Now she could enjoy the show.

The musical was delightful. Of course, it wasn't of the caliber of a New York production or the touring casts she'd seen in Houston, but what the students lacked in experience, they made up for in enthusiasm. And the dean was exceptional in his huckster role.

"This is great," Carrie said when the lights came on for intermission. "Makes me want to hop up on the stage, do a little soft shoe and belt out a song with the chorus."

Frank smiled. "I can't quite say it has that effect on me, but I'm enjoying it."

"Do you sing and dance?" Mary Beth asked.

"Used to when I was younger. Strictly amateur stuff—though I once dreamed of having a career on the stage. That was before I grew up and found out pursuing the bright lights was a good way to starve to death. But I was in a few productions in high school and college just for kicks."

"Did you ever do any community theater?" Frank asked.

Carrie shook her head. "It would be fun, but my work schedule is too erratic."

Mary Beth lifted an eyebrow and looked at Frank as if they might share an idea. "Are you thinking what I'm thinking?"

"What?" Carrie said, looking back and forth between them.

Mary Beth elbowed J.J. "Did you hear that Carrie is a singer and dancer?"

"Say, that's great."

"Whoa," Carrie said, laughing. "I didn't quite say that."

"If you can carry a tune at all and can do a shuffle step without falling over your feet, you're better than most of the people in Naconiche. You're going to be in town for at least three more weeks, aren't you?"

Puzzled, Carrie said, "I plan to be. At least that. What are you getting at?"

Mary Beth ignored the question. "Perfect. Don't you think she'll be perfect, Frank?"

"Perfect," he agreed. "For what?"

"Don't tell me that you've forgotten. The Fall Follies."

Frank groaned. "I'd forgotten."

"What is the Fall Follies?" Carrie asked.

"It's sort of a variety show," Frank said. "We do it every year to raise money for various community projects."

"The town's been doing it for years," Mary Beth said. "Nonie Outlaw is in charge."

"Which means," J.J. added, "that all the Outlaw clan gets roped into helping."

"Oh, don't complain, J.J.," Mary Beth said. "It'll be fun. Nonie says that our star tonight, Barry Bledsoe, is going to direct again this year. I've missed the last several years, but Nonie told me that he comes over and brings several student assistant directors. He puts together a show—usually songs from popular stage productions—and casts townspeople in various roles. Some are serious, some are played for laughs—and a lot of the acts are funny whether they're meant to be or not. Each act, under one of the assistants, rehearses like crazy for two weeks. Then we put it together at a dress rehearsal on Saturday morning and present it on Saturday night.''

''Why not have a dress rehearsal on Friday night? Wouldn't that be less hectic?''

''Friday night is for football,'' Frank said.

''Oh, of course,'' Carrie said, amused.

''Anyhow,'' Mary Beth said, ''it's going to be a blast. And if you're going to be here, you're a natural for a part. Come on, say you will. It'll be fun.''

''But I'll be working.''

''Most of us will be working,'' Frank said, ''but rehearsals are usually at night or after work, whatever's convenient for the members of the act.''

''Are you going to be in it?'' Carrie asked him.

He grinned. ''Mama would nail my hide to the wall of the Double Dip if I didn't show up for tryouts next week.''

''Tryouts?''

''That's a loose definition of the process,'' he said.

''Everybody who shows up is assigned a job—even if it's building the sets or passing out programs,'' Mary Beth said. ''Say you'll do it.''

''Let me think about it.''

''Think hard. I'm going to run to the ladies' room. Want to go?''

''I'll pass,'' Carrie said simply. She didn't even want to try to put on her shoes yet.

CARRIE LOST HERSELF in the second half of the performance and, at the end, clapped as hard as anybody for the cast. The actors were beaming as they took a second curtain call.

She was beaming as well. ''Fantastic,'' she said,

turning to Frank. "I love the way a show pumps me up. It's a great feeling, don't you think?"

"Absolutely. Ready to go?" he asked, motioning toward the people moving toward the exit.

Carrie looked down at her feet. She'd sooner have her fingernails ripped out with rusty pliers than to cram her feet back into those blasted shoes. "Uh," she said, "could we wait a minute until the crowd clears out?"

"Sure."

J.J. tapped Frank with his rolled-up program. "You folks ready to go?"

"We're going to wait a minute," Frank said. "Go ahead."

J.J. and Mary Beth were soon absorbed by the crowd. As Carrie watched them go, she tried to think of a way to handle her predicament gracefully. She finally decided to simply tackle the situation head-on. No way was she going to stick her feet into those torture devices again.

She picked up her shoes and stood. "I hope you don't mind if I go barefoot to the car. Seems I rubbed a blister on my foot."

"A blister? Where?"

"On my left foot. I think there are a couple of them."

"Let me see." He sat down. "Sit down and stick your foot up here." He patted his thigh.

"Frank, it's fine."

In an I'll-brook-no-nonsense judge's voice, he said, "Sit down and show me your foot."

She sat.

He patted his thigh again.

She propped her heel on it. And felt like an idiot as he examined it carefully.

"These are nasty," he said. "The one on your little toe is rubbed raw, and this big place on the ball needs to be protected. You don't want to get an infection. I don't suppose you have a couple of bandages in that purse, do you?" He nodded toward the small bag she carried which had barely enough room for a little cash, a credit card, her motel key and a lipstick.

She shook her head. "Sorry."

"I'll carry you to the car."

"Don't be ridiculous. You're not going to carry me all the way to the parking lot."

He stood. "I'll carry you."

She stood. "No," she said emphatically, "you will not."

"Yes," he said just as emphatically, "I will."

Setting her jaw, she glared up at him. "The matter is not up for negotiation."

"'Scuse me, folks," a voice said from the theater door. "We need to lock up."

"Give us a minute, please," Frank said sternly to the student who stood there.

"Yes, sir."

Frank patted his pockets. "Damn. I don't even have a handkerchief with me." He started tugging at his tie and ripped it off.

"What are you *doing?*"

"I'm making a bandage for a hardheaded woman."

"A bandage? With your tie? You can't do that. It'll ruin it."

He shrugged. "It's old, and I didn't like it much anyway. Sit down. Give me your foot."

She sat back down and stuck her heel back on his

thigh. Very carefully he wrapped the silk around her foot, then he retrieved a penknife from his pocket, split the small end tail and tied it securely.

She wiggled her big toe and admired his handiwork. "Very nice. It coordinates nicely with my outfit. You should have gone into medicine instead of law."

He chuckled. "I couldn't take the hours. But I've learned a little first aid over the years. That should protect the spots until we can get something to clean and bandage them properly." He stuck her shoes in his jacket pockets and offered his arm. "Ready?"

After he had her settled in the car, Carrie discovered that he wasn't kidding about cleaning and bandaging the blisters properly. He drove to an all-night drugstore, and she waited in the car while he went in and got supplies. He would have administered first aid in the parking lot if she hadn't insisted that they wait until she got back to her room.

The whole thing was actually very endearing. She couldn't remember the last time anyone took care of her.

"YOU'RE GOING TO *WHAT?*"

"I'm going to wash your foot," Frank said as he knelt in front of her with a pan of soapy water and one of clear.

The minute they were inside her room, he'd stripped off his jacket, rolled up his sleeves and gone to the kitchenette to rummage through the cabinet for pots. He had instructed her to sit again. She was beginning to feel like a beagle at obedience school.

"In the first place," Carrie said, "my foot won't fit in that pot. My size eights aren't in the Cinderella category. And in the second, I can wash my own foot.''

"You don't have to put your whole foot in," he said as he unwrapped the necktie bandage. "Just the front part." He rolled up her pants leg and guided her foot into the warm soapy water. "See?" He very gently bathed the abraded area, his touch no more than a petal over her skin.

She didn't want to admit that it felt like heaven.

He rinsed the area in the other pan of water and blotted it dry with a towel. Then he held up her foot to inspect the injury. He looked up at her and grinned. "This is the point where I always ask Janey if I should kiss the boo-boo and make it well."

She laughed. "I think we can safely skip that part."

"How about I put some of the antiseptic cream on instead?"

"Frank, I can do this. I've been taking care of my own cuts and scrapes for as far back as I can remember."

"Didn't your mom tend to them when you were a kid?" he asked, ignoring her protests and dabbing on the cream.

Carrie shook her head and tried to think of a coherent answer. The feel of his hands on her foot was extremely sensual. She stared at the painting across the room, doing her best to ignore the effects of his fingers on her. She'd never realized that feet were such powerful erogenous zones.

"My mother couldn't stand the sight of blood. A paper cut was enough to put her into orbit. Skinned knees and elbows were way too much for her."

"Did you have a lot of skinned knees and elbows?"

"Quite a few." She glanced down at him. His gaze met hers, and a zing raced over her. He had the most beautiful eyes.

Dark.

Magnetic.

Filled with…with something that bored into the core of her being and sent a wave of desire over her.

She quickly forced her attention back to the picture on the opposite wall, pasted a cheerful smile over the awestruck gape she felt and fumbled for the thread of their conversation. "What was I saying?"

"You were telling me about your many skinned knees as a kid."

"Oh, yes. I was a big tomboy—much to my mother's disappointment. She would have loved for me to be the ruffles and tea parties type, but I was a more rambunctious kid who preferred climbing trees to playing with Barbie. I guess that's why I blossomed when I went to live with Uncle Tuck and my cousin Sam. I could wear jeans and get as dirty as I wanted. I loved it."

"You didn't live with your mother?"

"Not from the time I was fourteen. But believe me, I was better off in a stable environment with my uncle. He was a wonderful influence in my life."

"Is he still living?"

"Very much so. I see him often."

He put the last piece of tape on the bandage and gave her foot a final pat. "That ought to take care of it. After you get in bed, you should probably take the wrapping off and let air get to those places. They'll heal in no time if you're careful." He stood.

She stood as well. "Thanks," she said, placing her hand on his upper arm. "You've taken very good care of me." She meant to move her hand after the casual touch. She really did. But her hand seemed content there against the strength she felt.

When she lifted her gaze to his again, he had that same look in his eyes, only this time it was even more visceral. The moment seemed to hang suspended in time.

"Carrie," he said, his voice husky.

"Yes?"

"I'm going to kiss you."

"I wish you would." Her voice was none too steady, either.

He lifted her chin with the back of his fingers, and she closed her eyes as he bent toward her. The first touch of his lips was a tentative brushing against hers.

She loved his lips. They were warm, full, gentle.

Then he gathered her into his arms and deepened the kiss. He groaned and put his heart and soul into it, and she responded in kind.

Dear Lord, he was so fine. She clutched handfuls of his shirt to keep from puddling at his feet.

She was just getting started when he broke away.

"I...I really enjoyed the evening," he said. "Now you need to get off that foot."

"My foot is fine," she said, lifting her mouth toward his again.

He dropped a quick kiss on her forehead instead of on the lips she blatantly offered. "Good night."

And then he was gone.

Out the door quicker than greased lightning.

She lifted her eyebrows and stared at the door that had closed behind him. "And good night to you, too, Judge."

## Chapter Seven

Dr. Kelly Martin flung open her blue door and grabbed Carrie in a bear hug. "I'm so glad you came," she said. "I can't tell you how excited I've been since I ran into you at aerobics class. It's good to see an old face."

"Not *that* old, I hope."

"Scratch old. Make that familiar face from days gone by."

Kelly had done well for herself, Carrie thought as her friend showed her around. She had a darling two-bedroom cottage near the hospital, beautiful furnishings and two cats of the alley variety.

"They're perfect pets for me. They pretty much take care of themselves. Plus they keep my feet warm at night."

"You mean the good doctor doesn't have a handsome man to warm her feet?"

Kelly snorted. "There are slim pickings around Naconiche. Almost all the good ones are married. The Outlaw brothers were the only eligible, desirable men around here over the age of thirty and under the age of retirement. Desirable being defined as someone who bathes regularly and can converse intelligently.

Mary Beth snagged one, and I understand you've captured the other.''

''Me? What are you talking about?''

''Sweetie, don't act innocent. The grapevine around here is faster than the Internet. Let's see, you and Frank Outlaw have had lunch together three, or maybe four, times this week. You were at the football game with him Friday night and went to the college musical in Travis Lake last night, *and* his car was parked outside your room for exactly nineteen minutes when he brought you home.''

''Wow,'' Carrie said. ''I'm impressed.''

Kelly chuckled and twirled an imaginary mustache. ''Zee doctor knows everything. Between the office and church this morning, I know most of what's going on in town. I hope you're as impressed by lunch. I love to cook, but I don't have much time for it anymore.''

''Don't worry about me. I'm the queen of frozen dinners.''

''Want to eat outside? The weather's perfect for it.''

''Great,'' Carrie said.

They heaped their plates with salad and southwestern chicken with corn salsa, and took trays outside to the patio table. The food was scrumptious.

''How long have you been in Naconiche, Kelly?''

''About two years. I came to take over the practice of a retiring doctor. While Naconiche doesn't have some of the advantages of city living, neither does it have the traffic and stress level. I really love it here.''

''Except for the lack of a decent dating pool.''

Kelly smiled. ''Right. But don't worry about me. There's a neurologist over in Travis Lake that I see occasionally—nothing serious. Now enough about me and my pitiful love life. I want to hear about yours.''

''What love life? I'm on the road most of the time, and guys seem to lose interest when you're gone for months at a time. Couple of times I've come home to find that my fella had gotten engaged to someone else while I was gone.''

''Bummer. But what's the skinny on Frank Outlaw?''

''No skinny,'' Carrie said. ''Most of the times people saw us together were mere happenstance, and we've only had one date. We went to that musical last night with J.J. and Mary Beth. Granted, the judge is a hunk, but I'll be gone to the next job in a few weeks. Say, I'm not cutting in on you by dating him, am I?''

''Heavens, no. I treat him and his whole family, and I've never even felt a twinge of romantic interest for Frank. And as far as I know, you're the only date he's had since his wife died.''

Carrie lifted her eyebrows over that but didn't comment.

''Tell me about what brings you to Naconiche,'' Kelly said. ''I heard someone say that you were a genealogist, but the last I heard you were in law school. Did your plans change?''

Carrie didn't say anything for a minute. She took time to sip her tea and pat her mouth with her napkin, wondering if she should confide in Kelly. Finally, she sat back in her chair. ''Not exactly.''

''Meaning?''

''Kelly, I've found myself in an awkward spot and I'd like to speak with you confidentially about it.''

Kelly raised her right hand. "On my honor as a doctor and a sorority sister, I won't breathe a word." 

Carrie smiled. "We don't have to get out the Bible." She explained about the oil leases and her real business in town.

"But why be so secretive about it?"

"I work for my uncle's company, a small independent outfit, and he's adamant about keeping a lid on this until I'm ready to start offering money and signing up landowners. Timing is critical. If some of his competitors get wind of it—"

"They'd run in and begin leasing the land out from under you," Kelly finished.

"Right. I often use the story about being a genealogist if I want to poke around courthouse records without letting them know I'm a landman until I'm ready."

"Pardon me," Kelly said, "but shouldn't that be landperson? Landman sounds very sexist."

Carrie laughed. "Doesn't it? But in this tough business, I'm lucky to be considered a good ole boy with breasts."

"Okay, so you're undercover. What's the big deal?"

"The big deal is that I don't usually mingle much with the locals. In Naconiche I have. And that may have been a mistake. The word sort of spread that I was a professional genealogist, and I had a hard time discussing my research interest without lying to people like Mary Beth and J.J. and Frank. Can you imagine how I agonized when they asked me about my work and how carefully I had to choose my words to keep from actually lying to a local sheriff and a judge?"

"Awkward."

"Beyond awkward," Carrie said. "And I have to keep it up for another couple of weeks. I'm beginning to feel like a mole living a secret life. I hate misleading people who are beginning to become my friends. I'm usually an up-front kind of person."

"But Carrie, this is all going to come out soon. I'm sure people will understand when you explain."

"You think so? I just discovered Friday that the Outlaw property is smack-dab in the middle of the prime unit."

"Uh-oh. You're afraid that the Outlaws might think you've been cozying up to them to get their leases."

"Yes, but it gets worse," Carrie said. "I almost confided in Frank last night, but I couldn't seem to bring myself to do it. Then this morning something I'd found in the records started nagging at me, and I called Uncle Tuck. Seems that several years ago, one of the big oil companies tried to lease land in the same general area, but they ran into a major snag with one family that screwed up the whole deal."

"Which family was that? Did he know?"

Carrie nodded. "The Outlaw family."

"Oh, dear. Big problem."

"You're telling me."

"Didn't your uncle warn you about a potential problem?"

"He didn't say a word, the stinker. But then he has an illogical faith in my ability to get anybody, anywhere to sign on the dotted line. He didn't want to prejudice me, so he didn't mention past unsuccessful ventures."

"I can see where things might get a little sticky,"

Kelly said. "But sooner or later you're going to have to tell the Outlaws the truth about who you are if you want to lease their land."

"There's a way around it. When I finish my research and locate all the property owners, I can hire an independent broker to do the actual leasing."

"And keep on with your phony front until you sneak out of town? That's not your style."

Carrie sighed. "You're right. I've got to come up with the right way to handle this without alienating anyone. I genuinely like these people, but at the same time, I have an ethical obligation to my job."

"There's a bright side to this," Kelly said.

"What am I missing?"

Kelly grinned. "I own ten acres adjoining the Outlaw property. Do you really think there's oil out there?"

Laughing, Carrie said, "Uncle Tuck thinks there's a good chance. Where is your property? I haven't seen your name on the tax roles."

"I have land all over the county, but the piece I'm talking about is just to the south and fronts County Road 117. It was part of Vernon Burrows's acreage, but he deeded it to me last spring for treating his whole family for the past two years. He has ten kids. I get some strange items as payment sometimes. Land is one of the nicer things."

"Did he deed you the mineral rights?" Carrie asked.

"I think so. I have the deed in my safe deposit box at the bank."

"Then if you have all or any part of the mineral rights, I'll want to sign you up because I discovered

Vernon Burrows last Friday, too. His property is in the unit I'm interested in.''

Kelly grinned. "How much are you offering, Ms. Landman?''

"A hundred dollars an acre for a five-year option. Interested?''

"Where do I sign?''

Carrie laughed. "I wish everybody would be this easy, but I have a funny feeling that this may be the hardest project I've ever tackled. As my uncle Tuck would say, I'm smack-dab on the horns of a dilemma.''

FRANK WAS IN A DILEMMA. Coming to the cemetery Sunday afternoon was hard, but he knew that he had to. Susan had been not only his wife and lover but his best friend.

He tossed the withered mums into a nearby trash barrel and laid a new bouquet of wildflowers by her headstone. He brushed away leaves and traced the letters of her name.

"Susan, I've met someone. A woman. I think you'd like her. Mary Beth does. And so do J.J. and Mama and Dad. I...I kissed her last night, Susan. And I enjoyed it. God, I'm so sorry.''

Susan's laughing face filled his mind and, remembering all the times he'd kissed her, his words to her echoed in his head. "I'll always love you,'' he'd told her countless times. "There'll never be another woman for me,'' he'd vowed. "Never.'' He stood quickly and walked away.

Guilt was eating him alive. The rational part of him said that Susan was dead, and he should get on with a normal life. But emotionally, he couldn't let her go.

She'd been the center of his existence for so long that it was impossible to turn from her. Until he'd first seen Carrie, Frank hadn't even been remotely stirred by another woman. His dreams had been of Susan. Now they weren't. He dreamed of Carrie. Like an obsession, Carrie filled his thoughts. She heated his blood and had him panting to get her in bed.

It's not as if theirs would be a permanent relationship, he rationalized. In a short time Carrie would be gone to do her research in some other town. Maybe just a casual affair—

He cursed his weakness and strode to his car. God, he hated what was happening to him. It would be best if he avoided Carrie Campbell completely.

LATE SUNDAY AFTERNOON when Carrie, singing along with a tune on the radio, turned into the entrance to the Twilight Inn, a car turned in behind her. Her heart did a flip-flop when she realized that the car was Frank's. She pulled into her slot and got out, expecting him to stop at her door.

He didn't.

Instead the car drove on to the office apartment. She stood there watching, mouth agape and feeling a little hurt.

The back door opened, and Janey jumped out. "Hi, Carrie!" she called, waving. "Daddy's taking Katy and Jimmy and me out for pizza. Wanna come?"

She didn't have a chance to reply before Frank unfolded himself from the driver's seat and nodded to her. "Janey, I'm sure Miss Campbell has more important things to do than eat pizza with a bunch of wild Indians."

Actually she wasn't very hungry after the big lunch

she'd had, but she would have appreciated the opportunity to speak for herself. Why did she have the distinct impression that the judge wasn't interested in her company? Maybe it was because the chill in his voice would freeze a well fire.

"Please, please, please," Janey begged her. "Do you like pepperoni? I do. Pepperoni with lots and lots of cheese."

"I'm more of a mushroom and olive person myself," Carrie told the child, "but I had a late lunch, and I couldn't do pizza justice. Thanks, anyhow."

"Daddy, make her co—"

"Janey," Frank said, "you'd better go get Katy so we can be on our way. Tomorrow is a school day." When Janey scampered inside, he said to Carrie, "Sorry about that. She gets a little exuberant sometimes."

"No problem."

She waited for him to say something else, but the silence became embarrassing. Then her embarrassment turned to irritation. You would have thought they were strangers. No one would have ever guessed that only last night he had kissed her more passionately than she'd ever been kissed in her life. She was savvy enough to realize that he was attracted to her, yet sometimes he acted very strange.

What was with the man?

Her temper flared. She didn't need the aggravation. Tossing a wave over her shoulder, she strode to her room.

As she unlocked the door, she glanced back at Frank. He was staring at her with a strange look in his eyes. *Dear Lord, you don't suppose that he's gotten wind that I'm not a professional genealogist?*

Guilt suddenly replaced her indignation.

No, she told herself. He would have said something. Maybe he simply had a headache or was tired. *Or maybe he wasn't as impressed with my kissing as I was with his.* No, she knew better than that.

Maybe he just felt a little shy and awkward with her around his kids.

In any case, she was going to have to tell Frank and the others why she was in town. And soon.

AT THE COURTHOUSE ON MONDAY Carrie found the record of Kelly's deed from Burrows. He had assigned her all the mineral rights to the small piece of his property that abutted the Outlaws'. She also discovered that Wes Outlaw had retained half the mineral rights to his large land holding, then had divided and deeded the land to each of his five children for "ten dollars and other considerations."

She estimated that, working hard, in a week and a half, she would have amassed all the information she needed before she began approaching the land owners for leases. Which meant that she had a week and a half to come clean with Frank.

Strange thing was, she didn't see or hear from Frank on Monday or on Tuesday. He wasn't at lunch at the tearoom either day. He hadn't called. Maybe he was out of town, she thought.

Carrie didn't spot Frank at the tearoom on Wednesday, either, but Ellen and Dixie from aerobics class were there and waved her over to join them.

Ellen kept them entertained with the story of an eccentric out-of-town client that she'd worked with for the past two days. "I swear that I'd rather deal with Clyde Burrows than that woman."

Carrie's antennae went up when she heard Clyde Burrows's name. He owned a large tract of property next to Vernon Burrows. "Who's Clyde Burrows?" she asked, doing her best to act casual.

"A local character," Ellen said.

"Crazy old coot," Dixie added.

"Is he mentally ill?" Carrie asked.

"No," Ellen said. "Not that I'm aware of. He's just cantankerous—and very peculiar. He lives alone in an old shack with about a dozen hunting dogs."

"How does he make a living?"

"I'm not sure," Ellen said. "I think he gets some sort of government pension."

"Clyde has only one eye," Dixie said. "I think he was wounded while he was in the army. Maybe that's what makes him so nasty. I heard that the Meals-on-Wheels bunch tried to sign him up for lunch delivery, and he ran them off with a shotgun."

Carrie's worry factor went up over that one. Great. Now she could look forward to contending with a trigger-happy nut. Oh, well, it wasn't the first time she'd had to deal with nuts. She was just glad that she'd been forewarned about this one.

"Mary Beth told us that you're a wonderful singer and dancer and that you're going to be in the Fall Follies," Ellen said.

Carrie shook her head. "I think my abilities have been exaggerated in the retelling. Years ago I liked to sing and dance, but I haven't done anything in ages."

"I'll bet you could pick it up in no time," Dixie said. "Ellen and I have always been in it—even when I was pregnant."

"Which was almost every year," Ellen added with a wink.

"My pregnant days are over," Dixie said. "Even my husband Jack is going to come to tryouts. You should come, Carrie. We need some fresh blood."

"I'm thinking about it," Carrie said. "Sounds like it might be fun. Now if you'll excuse me, ladies, I have to get back to my work. I enjoyed sharing lunch with you."

She paid her check and left.

Frank hadn't shown up during lunch. Carrie wondered again if he was out of town. Some juvenile impulse made her circle the courthouse looking for his car. There it was, parked in the back by the sheriff's patrol car.

Carrie was sure there was some perfectly logical reason for her not seeing him these past few days. A difficult docket perhaps. All sorts of possibilities came to mind, but one question kept coming up despite her reasonable explanations. The notion stung.

Was Frank deliberately avoiding her?

Why?

## Chapter Eight

Frank Outlaw had an attack of heartburn that wouldn't quit. He chalked it up to three days of eating chicken-fried steaks at the City Grill, and discreetly popped antacids while he listened to the afternoon's cases.

Funny, eating chicken-fried steaks had never bothered him before. He had a cast-iron stomach. Maybe as he was getting older his system was changing. Hadn't he heard his dad grumbling a hundred times about not being able to handle his favorite three-alarm chili anymore?

He started to yawn and quickly covered it by putting his fist to his mouth and clearing his throat. Lawyers didn't take kindly to inattentive judges—even if the one droning on now sounded like a bumblebee in a syrup bucket.

Frank dismissed the charges against the last defendant brought before him and was glad to call it a day. He hadn't had much sleep in the past few nights, either, and he was beat. Tonight he planned to hit the sack as soon as the twins were tucked in at eight-thirty.

His plans didn't quite work out.

Oh, he got to bed early—though a little later than eight-thirty. But his sleep was restless again. And he knew what caused the trouble. The trouble was named Carrie Campbell.

Avoiding her hadn't helped. And he was tired of running.

To hell with it. He was going to see her tomorrow.

After that he slept sounder than Scrub Peabody after a Saturday night toot.

BY THURSDAY Carrie had reached the conclusion that Frank was definitely avoiding her. Why, she didn't know. She vacillated between being ticked off and being relieved—ticked off that he would avoid her and relieved that she wouldn't have to keep up the charade.

If he didn't want to see her anymore, fine. She certainly wasn't going to lose any sleep over it. In fact, she'd make it easy for him. Since Frank, J.J. and Wes usually had lunch together at the tearoom on Thursdays, she opted for a sandwich in her room.

After she'd eaten, Carrie kicked off her shoes and sat cross-legged on the bed with her notes spread out around her. She planned to spend most of the afternoon getting organized and listing any gaps she needed to fill in. A couple of bugbears had shown up in her research, and being able to talk to someone who knew family lineage in the area surely would help. Maybe the time had come to talk to Millie at the library—if she could come up with the right tactic. She chewed on the end of her pen and tried to think of a good cover story that didn't stray too far from the truth.

Mulling over an idea, she reached for her glass of

soda on the nightstand and took a big swallow. A sudden knock on the door exploded like a shotgun blast and startled her so that the soda she was drinking went up her nose and most of the rest sloshed on her shirt and splattered on her papers.

Coughing and cursing, she bounded from the bed and ran to the bathroom for towels. Trying to salvage her work, she hurriedly blotted the array of papers on her bed.

There was another knock, even louder.

"Just a minute!" she screamed.

Throwing a clean towel over the mess on her bed, she grabbed another and dabbed at her shirtfront as she strode to the door, muttering and furious, and flung it open. "What the devil do you—"

There stood Frank Outlaw.

Maybe her scowl put him off because he waited a few beats before he said quietly, "We need to talk."

"So…talk. I'm listening."

He frowned and peered at her. "Have you been crying?"

Carrie shook her head. "No, I just snorted Coke up my nose."

His expression shifted to something between stunned and appalled.

Bursting into laughter, she said, "Not that kind of coke. The soft drink that comes in cans. Your loud knock startled me, and a swallow went the wrong way." She looked down at the dark stains wetting her shirt and held the towel over the disaster area.

"Sorry about that. Maybe we should start over."

"Sure." She closed the door.

There was a soft rap.

Carrie opened the door, and Frank stood there smiling.

"Hi," he said. "I've missed seeing you lately."

Her only response was a tiny nod acknowledging that she'd heard his words. She raised her brows slightly and waited for more.

"I...uh...I've had a full docket."

She nodded again. "Crime must be rampant in the county."

"Uh, yes. Well, I was wondering if you'd like to have dinner with me tonight."

"Oh, I'm sorry. Tonight is my aerobics class."

"How about tomorrow night? We could go to a movie."

"What about the football game?" she asked.

"It's an away game, but we could drive to Haskins to see it if you want to. It's about seventy-five miles away."

"Think I'll pass on the game." She didn't believe the story about the full docket and she was still miffed about his disappearing act. She didn't intend to make things easy for him.

"What about dinner and a movie?"

Effecting her best pondering expression, she was quiet for a minute.

"Dinner and miniature golf?"

She burst into laughter. "Miniature golf? I haven't played since I was about thirteen."

He grinned. "Naconiche has a remarkably challenging course. The windmill hole is especially formidable."

How could she resist that grin? Something about it had the power to fill her heart with sunshine. "You're on for dinner and miniature golf. Is there somewhere around here to get a good cheeseburger?''

''The Burger Barn. They have six kinds of burgers, French fries and the best onion rings in four counties.''

''I *love* onion rings.''

''Me, too,'' he said. ''Pick you up about seven?''

She nodded. ''Seven.''

When he left, she closed the door, leaned back against it and sighed. So much for playing hard to get. What was it about that man that could turn her into taffy in an instant?

WHEN FRANK got back to his car in front of the tearoom, he found J.J. leaning against the fender, his hat cocked back and a toothpick in his mouth.

''Well?'' his younger brother said.

''Well, what?''

''Did you ask her out again?''

''Ask who?''

J.J. snorted and shook his head. ''The lady in number five. Who the hell did you think I was talking about—the queen of England?''

''And what makes you think it's any of your business, little brother?''

''Swear to God, Frank, sometimes you're about as obstreperous as a sackful of rattlesnakes. She must have turned you down.''

''As a matter of fact, she didn't. We're going out tomorrow night.''

J.J. grinned. ''That ought to put you in a better mood.''

Frank shrugged. ''I've got to get back to the courthouse." He opened the car door, but J.J. didn't budge from the fender.

"Where you going?"

"I told you. To the courthouse."

"No, dang it. I meant where are you and Carrie going tomorrow night?"

Frank mumbled his answer and climbed in the car.

"What was that?"

"I said we're going to the Burger Barn and to play miniature golf—not that it's any of your blasted business."

J.J. hooted with laughter. "You're feeding her a hamburger? I can tell it's been a long time since you've asked anybody for a date, big spender. And *miniature golf?* Don't tell me you're taking the kids along."

"No, I'm not taking the kids. And she's the one who suggested a burger."

"I'll bet she didn't suggest putt-putt."

"Put a cork in it, J.J." Frank slammed the door and spun out of the parking lot. Now he not only felt guilty, he felt like a blamed fool.

THAT EVENING Carrie saw Millie going into the aerobics room just as she arrived, and she hurried to catch up and reintroduce herself. Millie was short and pear-shaped with gray beginning to show in her dark hair. She had one of those warm, sweet smiles that Carrie always associated with kindergarten teachers.

"Are you the expert librarian that everyone tells me I should consult?" Carrie asked.

"I'm not sure about the expert part, but I'm the librarian. You're the genealogist, aren't you?" Millie said.

Carrie smiled and said, "Among other things. I've been meaning to get by and talk with you about some of my research. Could I make an appointment to drop by the library tomorrow morning?"

"Oh, sure. I'll be happy to help any way that I can. We have quite an extensive collection of genealogical information for the county. But there's no need for an appointment. Drop by anytime after the library opens at nine."

"Great. I have some questions to ask about a couple of families—the Sangers and the Rushings."

"I'm sure I can help there. My mother was a Sanger, you know. And the Rushings first came to the county in eighteen fifty-seven. Or was it fifty-eight? I can check in the morning. It won't take a jiffy."

Others began arriving, and Carrie greeted them, already feeling like a friend to Mary Beth, Ellen and Dixie. And Kelly of course.

Just as Mary Beth started to the front of the room, Kelly said, "Stay for a minute after class, will you? I want to ask a favor."

Carrie nodded, then the music and sweating started.

When the hour was up, Carrie mopped her face and waited for Kelly. Kelly seemed to hesitate until most of the others were gone. Finally Dixie and Ellen walked outside and only Mary Beth was left with them.

"Would you two like to come over for a cold drink and snack?"

"Maybe in a sec," Kelly said. "I need to talk to Carrie for a minute. We'll lock up here."

"No problem," Mary Beth said. "Just twist the lock on the doorknob. We'll be over at the tearoom."

When Mary Beth had gone, Carrie asked, "What's the deal?"

"Nothing major, but I need a favor. Saturday is the day for Fall Follies tryouts, and I promised Miss Nonie that I would participate this year. Problem is, I can't commit to spending a lot of time practicing with a group since I'm always on call, and I have a couple of babies due about that time. Then I remembered that revue we did in college, and you were so great in it. I thought maybe we could do that one at tryouts and for the show as well."

"Which one?"

"The 'Diamonds' number."

Carrie chuckled. "Lord, I'd forgotten about that. I don't think I can even remember the words to the song."

Kelly grinned. "I've got that problem solved." She reached into a bag at her feet and pulled out a sheet of paper. "My receptionist found the words on the Internet. And here is the soundtrack," she added, retrieving two objects from the bag. "I have cassette and CD. I know the routine will come back to you as soon as you listen a couple of times. It did to me. Will you give it a go? I think it would be a kick."

"Oh, Kelly, I don't know. I wasn't planning on participating in the show. And anyhow, we had six or eight girls in that number."

"This is just for the tryouts Saturday. We could add some more people later. You could teach them the routine. Pretty please?"

Carrie laughed at Kelly's childlike expression. "What will your patients think of you after we do this?"

"That I'm a human being—and a darned good sport with nice legs. Is that a yes?"

"Only for a sorority sister. But we need at least one practice session before we make idiots of ourselves."

"How about tomorrow night?" Kelly asked.

"Got a date."

Kelly quirked a brow. "With Frank?"

Carrie nodded. "What about now?"

"I have to make rounds at the hospital. How about lunchtime tomorrow? My office. Twelve-thirty. I'll have Ginny pick up something for us to eat."

"I'll be there."

"Let's keep this a surprise for now," Kelly said as they left. "I may get cold feet."

"After you've wheedled me into doing it? No way."

Carrie stopped by her room to drop off the items Kelly had given her and went to join the ladies for munchies.

She was glad she did. Mary Beth had some scrumptious peach cobbler, and she thoroughly enjoyed the girl talk. Dixie was a stitch, and Ellen was a sharp lady. In fact, since Ellen was in real estate, Carrie decided to give some thought to having Ellen help her with the leases when she was ready for that phase of her project.

"Have you decided to be in the Fall Follies?" Mary Beth asked Carrie.

"I think I may. How exactly does the process work?"

"Like a zoo," Dixie said.

"Near enough," Ellen said. "Some people go with real tryout material, others just show up. Barry has been doing this for so long that he's familiar with what most people can do. The three of us have been discussing having something prepared this year. That might be kind of fun.''

''Unless it's one of the novelty numbers from *Funny Girl,* don't count on me,'' Dixie said. ''You know I can't carry a tune in a bucket. Even the church choir won't let me do anything more than press their robes and stoles.''

''I'll leave you to figure something out,'' Carrie said. ''I'm pooped.'' She said her goodbyes and went back to her room.

Once she'd showered and had on her nightshirt, she put the CD into her portable player, listened to the movie soundtrack and read over the words to the song. Just as Kelly had predicted, the old routine came back to her. She ran through the number a couple of times, singing quietly and practicing the steps. She even remembered most of the girls who were a part of it: Kelly, Leah Jenkins, Liz Wannamaker, Wanda Davis and Nita something-or-the-other, the tall blonde from Amarillo. Carrie still saw Liz, who lived in Houston, for lunch occasionally when she was home. The last she'd heard, Leah was married to an actor on a TV soap and lived in New York. She'd lost track of the others. A shame really. Once they'd all been so close. But friendships with women, like relationships with men, were hard to maintain when you didn't have time to devote to them. After the last few days in Naconiche and the budding friendships she'd found, she was beginning to realize how much she'd been missing.

It bothered her that she couldn't remember Nita's last name.

On a whim, she telephoned Liz Wannamaker, rather Liz Owen now. Liz would know. She went to reunions and kept up with all that stuff.

But she couldn't reach Liz at the old number. She got a recording that told her the number had been changed. Carrie didn't even recognize the area code. Lord, she didn't know Liz had moved. How long since she'd seen her?

When she thought about it, their last lunch had been over a year ago. A *year?* Good grief. Feeling a little blue over the pitiful state of her social life, she climbed under the covers and turned on the TV news.

THE NEXT MORNING Carrie arrived at the library at nine-fifteen and found Millie waiting for her with two loose-leaf binders and a couple of CDs.

"I went ahead and pulled the family histories of the Sangers and the Rushings. The binders are for library use only, but you can check out the CDs if you like. That is, if you have a computer with you. I thought you might like to look through the binders first to see if any of the information is what you're looking for."

"Oh, Millie, thanks. I'll get right on it. And yes, I have a laptop with me. I'd be lost without it."

"Before you start, let me show you where we keep our other genealogical materials, including the name index of most of the past and present citizens of the county."

"You're a sweetheart to do this."

Millie smiled shyly. "It's all part of my job. And genealogy has been my passion for years. My mother, God rest her soul, got me interested when I was just a girl. It's so good to meet a professional. How long have you been in the field?''

''For only a few years. I'm sure I'm a neophyte compared to you. By the way, I brought my copy of your book along for you to autograph. I really enjoyed reading it.''

Millie actually blushed. ''Thanks. I'd be happy to sign it.'' After she had autographed the fly page, Millie said, ''I'll leave you to your research. Let me know if you need anything else.''

Carrie took her briefcase and the materials to a table and started glancing through the binders. In no time at all, she had the information she needed to locate names of heirs to retained mineral rights of the properties in question. And interestingly, it seemed that Millie and her brother Carl might each own quarter shares in a large tract of land in the unit she was after. That done, she checked other names on her list with those in the library index. All of them were there. She looked through several of the binders, making notes of particulars here and there and deciding which CDs she wanted to check out for the weekend.

Including the one of the Outlaw clan.

Finding this information was like hitting a gusher. These family histories would save hours and hours of tedious work. She could kick herself for not tapping this source sooner. She should have listened. Hadn't everybody in town told her that she ought to talk to Millie at the library?

By the time Carrie came up for air, it was nearing noon. She had just enough time to stash her materials in her room and freshen up for her lunch and practice session with Kelly.

Feeling lighthearted as she drove back to the Twilight Inn, she began singing the number they would be rehearsing, bobbing and twisting to the beat. When she stopped at a light, a grizzled old man in a rusty pickup truck looked at her strangely. She only smiled and waved and kept singing. He smiled and waved back.

With her new laminated Naconiche library card and plans to participate in the town Follies, she was beginning to feel like a citizen of this place.

Nah, Carrie told herself. Small towns were stifling after a while. She was anxious to finish this assignment and go home. She planned to take some time off and do all the things she enjoyed doing in the city—shopping in the Galleria, seeing plays at the Alley Theater, eating Thai food, enjoying performances at the Music Hall, visiting the museums, playing·golf at Champions or the Woodlands.

How long since she'd taken time to play even nine holes of golf? And it used to be her passion.

She smiled. At least she'd get to practice her putting tonight.

# Chapter Nine

"Dad gum it!" Frank said as he nicked himself again. That was the second time he'd cut himself shaving. He was as nervous as a cricket in a henhouse.

"That's not a nice word, Daddy," Janey said from her perch on the counter between the double sinks.

"I know, sweetheart, and I'm sorry." He dabbed at the blood with a towel, but the little spot on his Adam's apple kept gushing like a son of a gun.

"You have to hold a tissue on the place 'til the blood stops," Janey said, sounding more like a mother than a five-year-old. She plucked a tissue from the box near her and folded it neatly, then got on her knees and held the square against his throat. "Why are you so cross?"

"Am I cross? I didn't mean to be." He stood patiently and waited while Janey held the compress.

"Maybe it was because you didn't eat your dinner. Matilda says if we don't eat our dinner our blood goes crazy. Is that why you're bleeding?"

Frank smiled. "No. I'm bleeding because I cut myself by not being careful enough. And I didn't eat because I'm going out to dinner with a friend."

"Who?"

"With Miss Campbell."

Janey brightened. "Carrie? The lady with the pretty eyes. I like her. She was a cheerleader. Is she going to be our new mommy?"

The question stunned Frank. "Of course not. Where did you get such an idea?"

"Matilda said one of these days you were going to bring home a nice lady to be our mommy."

"Looks like I'm going to have to talk to Matilda about this. I'm going out with Carrie...Miss Campbell because she's a visitor to town and doesn't have a lot of friends here."

Janey nodded soberly. "That's a very nice thing to do. I wish she'd gone to get pizza with us. Maybe we can invite her to come eat dinner here with us one night. We could watch a video, too. Would you ask her?"

"Maybe. Do you think the bleeding has stopped yet?"

Janey carefully lifted the folded tissue, squinted and stared at the wound for several seconds. "It's starting to ooze again." She slapped the compress back against his throat.

"I need to finish shaving," Frank said. "Tell you what. Why don't we tear off a tiny piece of tissue and put it on my cut?"

"Will that work?"

"I think so. Let's give it a try." He tore off a scrap of toilet tissue and plastered it on the cut.

"It's getting all bloody!"

Jimmy strolled into the room. "What's getting all bloody?"

"Daddy's neck. He put toilet paper on it and it's getting all bloody."

"Let me see," Jimmy said, climbing onto the counter beside his sister.

Frank kept shaving while Jimmy stared at his neck. "Oooo. Neat. How'd you do that, Daddy?"

"It was an accident, son."

"Why are you shaving now?" Jimmy asked. "You always shave in the morning."

"Because Daddy wants to look nice, stupid," Janey said. "He's going to keep Carrie from being lonely because she doesn't have any friends to eat with."

"Janey, don't call your brother stupid. And you should call her Miss Campbell."

"She told me I could call her Carrie."

"Who's Carrie?"

"Don't you remember? She's the lady with the pretty eyes. She was at the football game."

Jimmy shrugged. "Why doesn't she have any friends? Is she rude to people or something?"

Janey heaved an exaggerated sigh. "No, silly. She's a visitor. Daddy, it's getting really, really bloody."

Frank made a final swipe, then put down his razor and removed the tissue. After he rinsed his face and dried it, he put another piece of tissue on the cut. "Legs up," he told the twins so he could look in the center drawer for a styptic pencil.

Naturally he found everything except what he was looking for—even a little screwdriver that he'd lost months ago and an extra key to the riding mower that he'd combed the place for.

"What are you looking for, Daddy?" Janey asked, her nose in the drawer.

"A styptic pencil, but I can't seem to find one."

"What's a styp-tic pencil?" Janey asked.

"It's a little medicated stick that stops bleeding."

"You remember, Janey," Jimmy said. "It's that thing we used when we pulled the ticks off Bus—" Quickly, he clamped both hands over his mouth.

"You used my styptic pencil on the dog?"

"It worked real good."

"I'm sure it did. Out, you two. I need to finish getting dressed or I'll be late." Frank swung Janey down from the counter while Jimmy jumped down by himself and scampered from the bathroom.

"Daddy," Janey said, hanging back, "can I help you pick out a shirt?"

"Sure." Frank slapped aftershave on his face and gave his hair a couple of swipes with his brush.

Janey marched to his closet, rummaged through his shirts, then held out the sleeve of one. "Wear this."

The one Janey picked was a purplish dress shirt she'd given him for his birthday. It wasn't his usual style. "Why that one?"

"It's my favorite color," she said, "and it's the same color as Carrie's eyes. You'll look very handsome in it."

Her smile was so angelic and her expression so innocently expectant, that he didn't have the heart to tell her no. "Thanks for your help, sweetpea. Now scoot."

He put on the shirt, tucked it into his khakis and gave his loafers a final wipe with a damp towel. Glancing at his watch, he saw that he'd better get a move on or he'd be late.

CARRIE HAD a hard time deciding what to wear. Exactly what was the proper dress for hamburgers and miniature golf? She finally decided on khakis, a long-sleeved violet shirt and loafers.

Too preppy? she wondered as she studied herself in the mirror. Would jeans be better? The question was moot, for just then there was a knock.

When she went to the door, she took one look at Frank and started to laugh.

"Is it that bad? Janey picked the shirt, and—"

"No, no," Carrie said. "I like your shirt. It's not every man who can carry off violet, and you look very nice. I was laughing because we look like twins."

He grinned. "So we do. Great minds."

"Have an accident?" she asked, touching her own neck where a piece of tissue was stuck to his.

"Oh, God, is that still there?" He ripped off the white scrap. "Sorry. The twins used my styptic pencil on Buster."

"Who's Buster?"

"Our golden retriever."

"It's started bleeding again," she told him. "Come in and we'll use mine."

"You have a styptic pencil?"

"Sure, I'm always maiming myself when I shave my legs." She took his hand and led him to the vanity in the bathroom where she rummaged through her makeup case until she found what she was looking for. "Voilà!" she said, holding up the stick. He reached for it, but she said, "I'll do it."

She positioned him against the sink so that the light was good, and he spread his legs to make himself shorter and tilted his head back to give her better access to his neck. As she gently cleaned the place with a warm cloth, she became overwhelmingly aware of his sharp male scent. A wonderful kind of heat seemed to radiate from him, and she felt her pulse accelerate.

His Adam's apple bobbed, and a line of blood began to blossom there. She quickly blotted it dry and dabbed the spot with the dampened pencil. Sometime during the process, his arms had gone around her hips, and he pulled her closer. Not moving, she continued to stare at the treated spot. For several seconds he didn't move, either.

Slowly his chin came down, and their eyes met. "All done?" he asked.

"All done."

"Thanks," he murmured. "Ready to go eat?"

"Yes."

Still neither of them moved. Sensual awareness hung in the air like the room was full of steam.

"Hungry?" he asked.

"Very." She licked her lips.

"Me, too." He licked his.

He finally closed his eyes and took a deep breath. "We'd better get a move on. I wouldn't want to lose our reservations at the Burger Barn."

The mood was broken, and she laughed.

She slipped the pencil into its plastic sleeve and handed it to him. "Keep it. It's new and I have another."

"Thanks." He straightened and pocketed it.

Even though their conversation turned to mundane subjects, the awakened intensity stayed with them as they drove to the hamburger place. There was no denying that Frank Outlaw turned her on like blue blazes, and it was pretty obvious that he felt the same. While she'd never been into casual sex, she was seriously considering making an exception. She wondered if he carried protection.

*Get off that track!* she told herself. They were simply going to share a meal and have a few laughs while they knocked a ball around a hokey little course. No more.

THE BURGER BARN was appropriately named. It was a big barn of a place, painted rusty red, with a lot of weathered wood inside and decorative farm items on the walls. Smoky odors of grilling meat permeated the air. It was also dim and noisy. The place was full, and the *ding-dings* and electronic blips of video machines mixed with scores of conversations punctuated with an occasional shout or burst of laughter.

"It's bedlam," Frank said against her ear. "Especially on weekends. But their burgers are great."

A chunky teenager in skintight jeans met them with a pair of menus. She beamed at Frank. "I saved you a table, Judge. It's in a corner out in the annex where it's a little quieter."

"Thanks Patsy Jo," he said.

They followed as Patsy Jo led them through the obstacle course of people and tables and kids running around.

The annex, a long enclosed porch with banks of windows, was quieter. Marginally.

"What can I getcha to drink?" Patsy Jo asked.

They settled on light drafts, and she left them with menus.

"I thought you were teasing about the reservations," Carrie said.

"Only partly. They don't really take reservations here, but Patsy Jo and I go way back."

Carrie raised her brows and waited for an explanation.

"Let's just say that we had a previous professional connection, and she's made some positive directional changes."

Amused, she nodded. "Sounds like you bailed her out of some trouble."

"You could safely say that." He opened his menu. "What looks good to you?"

"Everything. And the smells have my mouth watering." She finally decided on a cheeseburger with grilled mushrooms and onions.

"That sounds good to me, too," Frank told the waitress after Carrie ordered. "And bring us a large order of fries and another of onion rings."

Frank took a swallow of his beer, then asked, "How is your research coming?"

This was the perfect opening, Carrie thought. She could very casually explain what her real job here was. She started to, then for some reason hesitated. First it might be wise to ask around and find out why the Outlaws had opposed leasing for oil exploration before.

"I met with Millie and spent the morning at the library," she said, then related her surprise and delight at the extensive genealogy collection.

"Millie is a real asset to this town," Frank said. "She's almost the stereotypical old-maid librarian, but in her younger days she wanted to be an opera singer."

"An opera singer?"

Frank nodded. "She has a beautiful voice. But her father died when she was in college and her mother became very ill. She stayed home and cared for her mother until she died, taking a few courses along at the college in Lake Travis. After her mother died, it was too late to follow her dream, but she finished her degree in whatever librarians get degrees in and took over our local library, which was in sad shape. She almost single-handedly transformed the place into what it is today."

"She's done a fine job."

Their food arrived, and the aromas from the luscious-looking feast set her stomach growling. "Oops," she said, slapping her hand over her tummy. "Sorry about that."

He grinned. "You said you were hungry. Dig in."

She did. Everything was yummy. "I swear this is the best cheeseburger that I've had since I ate at Otto's in Houston a couple of years ago. This may be my quota of calories and cholesterol for a month, but I don't care."

"I figure that I'm about two or three years ahead from just this week," he said.

"How so?"

"From all the chicken-fried steaks I ate at—"

Ahh, she thought. And the devil made her grin and say, "The ones you ate at City Grill while avoiding me at the tearoom?"

"Avoiding you? Of course not. I've just been too busy to do more than just grab a quick bite on the run."

It appeared that Frank had tried his best to feign innocence, but he wasn't having much luck. He really *had* been avoiding her, she thought, and she wasn't going to be socially correct and let him weasel out of it.

"I don't buy it," she said. "I'm pretty sure you've

deliberately avoided me for several days. The question is—why? Have I offended you in some way?"

He shifted uneasily. "Offended me? Lord, no." He rubbed his forehead with two fingers, then said, "The truth is, Carrie, that I haven't dated in years—no one since my wife died—and I'm feeling a little conflicted about it. It's awkward for me. And kind of scary."

Feeling enormously relieved, she smiled and reached across to touch his hand. "I won't bite."

He grinned. "Cross your heart?"

She made an X on her chest.

The tension seemed to melt, and they ate and talked and had a wonderful time. Carrie even played a couple of the machines in the arcade before they left. She wasn't nearly as adept as the preteen boy on the machine beside hers.

Full and happy as they walked to the car, their arms went naturally around each other's waists.

"We don't really have to play miniature golf," Frank said. "We can drive over to Travis Lake and see a movie. There are some showing that got good reviews."

"Afraid I'll beat you?" she asked.

"On my home course? No way."

"Let's go check out that windmill hole. And be prepared. I intend to win."

"Want to make a small wager?" he asked.

"Dollar a hole."

He grinned. "You're on."

BY THE TIME they reached the windmill on the tenth hole, Carrie was ahead by four dollars.

"Why do I have the feeling that I've been hustled?'' Frank asked. I thought you said you hadn't played miniature golf since you were a kid.''

"I haven't," she said, studying the layout of the hole, "but I'm a pretty good putter on a regular course." She took her first shot, but her timing was off and the windmill blade deflected her ball.

"Ah, that explains it. You're a golfer." Frank's shot went through the opening perfectly, crossed a little babbling brook and rolled within inches of the hole.

"One of my mother's husbands was a pro. He taught me. And when I went to live with my uncle, I kept it up. He's a real golf nut. Do you play?" Her second shot made it through the opening, then plopped in the water. "Rats!"

"When I get a chance. Obviously I'm a little rusty." He tapped his ball into the hole.

"But a killer on the windmill hole. I'll give you this one. What did I do wrong?" She picked her ball out of the water and shook it off. Her goof must have been a common one since there was a roll of paper towels hanging on a nearby post.

Frank ripped off a sheet of paper and handed it to her. "The secret is to go through the exact center of the opening. If you veer to one side or the other, you go in the water."

"Ah. Next time I'll know."

They walked to the next hole where a teenage couple was playing. The girl was obviously inexperienced because the boy was standing with his arms around her trying to teach her how to stroke. Or maybe the girl wasn't so inexperienced after all; the cuddling looked like fun.

If Carrie had had any sense, she would have played

dumb and gotten the same "instructions." Or maybe she should blow a few holes and let Frank win. Carrie's mother used to scold her for being so competitive with boys. "The male ego is a delicate thing," Amanda always said.

But Carrie wasn't cut out for pandering to male egos. She played to win. When the couple moved on, she set down her ball and hit a hole in one.

"Great!" Frank said. "You win a free game."

And darned if she didn't feel proud of herself.

He took two shots, and she was still ahead by four bucks.

On the twelfth hole, Frank started to get serious, and soon they were neck and neck. She made another hole in one on eighteen to win by one dollar.

"Pay up," she said sticking out her hand.

He laughed and peeled a bill from his money clip. "I've never welshed on a bet yet. What's your handicap on a regular course?"

"I used to be a scratch golfer, but since I don't play frequently anymore, I think it's about a six."

"Sounds like we might be evenly matched. There's a really fine course just outside Travis Lake, and I belong to the club. Want to play tomorrow morning?"

"Oh, I'd love to, but tomorrow is Fall Follies tryouts. Had you forgotten?"

"I had. And my mother will skin me if I don't show up," he said. "How about Sunday afternoon?"

"I'd love it. I even have my clubs in the trunk of my car. Regrettably they haven't seen daylight in weeks."

He grinned. "Trying to hustle me again?"

She smiled. "Dollar a hole?"

"It's a deal. Want to go somewhere for a cup of coffee?"

"Sure."

Unfortunately the only places they found open in Naconiche were a truck stop, a beer joint on the highway and the Burger Barn, which was even more crowded than before and sure to be noisier.

"Tell you what," Carrie said. "I make a mean cup of coffee. Let's go to my room."

He hesitated for a moment, then said, "Fine by me. But I can't stay too long or…"

She laughed. "Or somebody will be timing how long your car was outside my room?"

"Ridiculous, isn't it? But that's a small town for you."

"I know. Maybe we can prop the door open."

"Can't. Bugs."

"Maybe we can safely push it to twenty minutes this time."

He frowned. "Twenty minutes?"

"Kelly told me word was around town last week that your car was parked outside my door for nineteen minutes."

"Maybe I can park around back."

That idea didn't work out. J.J., Mary Beth and Katy were getting out of J.J.'s pickup in front of unit one just as Frank's car pulled into the drive of the Twilight Inn.

"Curses," Frank said.

"Foiled again," Carrie added.

After they parked and got out, Mary Beth waved to them. "We were about to have some coffee and dessert over at the tearoom. Join us?"

Carrie was tempted to say no. She wanted to drag

Frank Outlaw into her room and jump his bones. But that probably wasn't wise. She and Frank glanced at each other, then said, "Sure," at the same time.

And they enjoyed being with J.J. and Mary Beth.

Katy had curled up and gone to sleep in one of the booths. When it was time to go, J.J. lifted her and carried her to Mary Beth's unit while Frank walked Carrie to the door of number five.

"I really enjoyed myself tonight," she said when they reached the door. "It was fun."

"Could I come in for a moment? I'd like very much to kiss you, and I don't want to do it out here in front of God and everybody."

She chuckled and led him inside. Once the door was closed, she turned and waited.

It wasn't a long wait. He took her into his arms and kissed her like a starving man at a feast. She responded just as eagerly.

In no time they were both breathing hard, and his palms cupped her bottom and pulled her tightly against him. She pulled his shirt out of the back of his pants and ran her hands inside to touch his skin, grinding herself even closer to him.

He groaned and pulled away. "I think we'd better stop before this goes too far."

"Speak for yourself," she said, pulling down his head and reaching for his mouth with hers.

His hand went between them, and he stroked her breasts before he wrenched away again. "I don't have any protection with me. Do you?"

She shook her head. "But you can be sure I'm going to the drugstore tomorrow."

He chuckled. "That ought to raise a few eyebrows. Let me handle it." He dropped a quick kiss on her nose. "I really did have a great time tonight—even if you did beat the pants off me."

She grinned and looked down at his khakis. "Not quite."

He laughed and kissed her nose again. "At miniature golf. Will I see you tomorrow at the tryouts?"

"I'll be there. Kelly and I have a routine worked out."

"I'll be looking forward to it." He started to kiss her again, then stopped. "I'd better go."

He tucked in his shirt, wiped lipstick from his mouth and left.

Carrie could only sigh.

*What a man.*

# Chapter Ten

Carrie had awakened that morning with a terrible dream that had her hyperventilating. She had dreamed that she and Kelly were on stage, they couldn't remember the words to their song and the audience started to boo and throw golf balls at them. Was she nervous or what?

Why had she ever let Kelly talk her into this? She hadn't performed in front of people for years. If her friend hadn't already gone to so much trouble and expense, Carrie would call and back out. But not only had Kelly—rather, one of the girls in her office—located a good karaoke version of their number so that they could sing along to the original music without the vocals, but she had also provided matching black spandex leggings, black T-shirts and long gloves, top hats, canes and enough junk rhinestone jewelry to send every cheap hooker in Tijuana into ecstasy.

And this was just for the tryouts. Heaven only knew what their final costumes would look like.

She put on the leggings and T-shirt, topped the garb with an oversize camp shirt and put the rest of the stuff into a tote bag—except for the cane and hat. She also opted to put her black high-heeled pumps into the tote and wear loafers.

When everything was ready, Carrie checked her watch. "It's show time!"

She had a stomach full of bees as she loaded her things into her car and headed for the high school auditorium. Although she had sung the song at least two dozen times and knew the words perfectly, her dream made her jumpy enough to shove the cassette into the car player and run through it a couple of times more.

And wouldn't you know—when she stopped at a light, the same old geezer in the rusty pickup pulled up next to her. Winking, he touched the brim of his battered cap with one finger, and a toothless grin spread over his face. She laughed, waved and kept singing. She could hear his cackle as she pulled away.

Carrie and Kelly had agreed to arrive early, hoping to do their routine before it got too crowded. But as she pulled into the parking lot at the school, it looked as if a lot of other people had had the same idea. She only hoped her knees didn't knock or her voice break. A pity she hadn't developed a severe case of laryngitis. Or that her foot blisters had healed so quickly.

But truthfully, a little part of her was relishing the notion of performing—the ham part of her that loved climbing onto a stage and giving her all to a Broadway tune. Trying to make it in show business was a tough road, and she ordinarily didn't regret making a stab at it when she was younger, but every now and then a little pang of "what if" crept in. She thought about Millie and wondered if the librarian ever lamented her choices. Singing in the church choir wasn't the same as singing at the Met—though Millie might never have made it in the big time.

Carrie pushed all her ruminations aside. Spending too much time "what iffing" only gave you a headache. She grabbed all her paraphernalia and struck out for the auditorium.

It took a moment for her eyes to adjust to the dimness of the place, but she saw several people clustered around the front. A quartet in straw hats was on the stage singing "By the Light of the Silvery Moon." Great harmony, she thought as she made her way down the aisle. About halfway down, she stopped dead still and gaped at the singers.

It was the Outlaw family: Miss Nonie, Mr. Wes, J.J. and *Frank.* And they were darned good. She crept closer and scooted into an aisle seat to listen to the rest. Wes sang a wonderful rumbling bass while Miss Nonie took the tenor part, and the two sons added their rich, clear baritones.

When the Outlaws were finished, everybody clapped, and Miss Nonie stepped to the apron of the stage where a mike was set up. "Thanks to Barry for letting us try out early," she said, "for I have a million things to do to get ready for the annual Naconiche Fall Follies. Now I'll turn the floor over to Barry Bledsoe, our director."

While Barry made his way to the mike, Carrie went down front to where Kelly was frantically waving to her.

"We're up next," Kelly said. "One of my mothers-to-be just got to the hospital. She's only four centimeters dilated, but I don't want to be late for the occasion. Come on backstage and let's finish getting our stuff on. I already gave Barry our tape."

They hurried backstage while Barry greeted those gathered and made opening remarks. While she was slipping on her heels and draping herself with jewels, Carrie heard him say that this year's theme was "Music through the Years" and would highlight songs and other acts representing various decades since the founding of the town.

"For example," he said, "the song the Outlaws just sang would be the early nineteen-hundreds. And the number we're about to hear is from a popular movie from the fifties, as well as a Broadway show that first opened in nineteen forty-nine—close enough to the fifties. Carol Channing starred in the Broadway hit, and Marilyn Monroe played Lorelei Lee in *Gentlemen Prefer Blondes.* And please note that the version of the song that's coming up predated the one in the Aussie *Moulin Rouge* by over fifty years.

"I'd better get on with it. One of the ladies trying out—and neither of the two is blond by the way—has to get to the hospital and deliver a baby. Dr. Kelly Martin and Miss Carrie Campbell."

"My teeth are chattering," Kelly whispered.

"Too late now," Carrie told her as she plunked the cheap top hat on her head. "It's show time!" She led the way to center stage and cued the music with a nod.

They took their places, and when the music came up, they strutted around the stage and belted out a sassy rendition of "Diamonds Are a Girl's Best Friend." They didn't make a single bobble from the first note to the last provocative wink and cock of their hats.

The small group gathered burst into enthusiastic applause, including Barry who was smiling and clapping as he walked toward them. "Fantastic, ladies. Just fantastic."

"Thanks," Carrie said as they all walked offstage. "We were thinking that if you wanted to put the number in the show, maybe we could add some other people."

"I want to use it for sure, but I think it's perfect with just the two of you. Is that okay?"

"Fine with me," Kelly said, snatching a small device from her waistband and looking at it. "Uh-oh. I've gotta get to the hospital. Call you later, Carrie." She hurried away.

"Have you done any work professionally?" Barry asked.

"Singing and dancing, you mean? No, but I thought about giving it a shot when I was younger." She smiled. "I became a lawyer instead."

"A lawyer?" she heard someone say behind her. When she turned, Frank was standing there, and her stomach balled into a tight knot. "I didn't know you were a lawyer. And I didn't know you could sing and dance like that."

"I guess it never came up. And speaking of singing," she said quickly, "I didn't know you and your family were singers."

He grinned. "I guess it never came up."

Barry looked back and forth between them. "I take it you two know each other." When they nodded, he said, "Don't go away. I was considering a song that would make a great duet, but I couldn't think of anybody in town that would fit the parts and could carry it off. Hang around for a few minutes, and I'll get back to you about it. Okay?"

"Sure," Frank said.

"Okay by me," Carrie added, slipping off her heels and putting on her loafers and her camp shirt.

After Barry left, Frank said, "That was a dynamite performance. And sexy as the dickens."

She shot him a cheeky grin as she took off her fake diamonds and dropped them into her tote. "Wait until you see us in full costume."

"What are you wearing?"

"Truthfully, since Kelly's receptionist is making our outfits, I'm not exactly sure. If they're like our old ones, they'll be short, satin and have a lot of fringe."

He looked puzzled. "What old ones?"

"The ones we had in college. Come to think of it, they'll probably be a bit more demure than the old ones, or we might scandalize the town."

"I can hardly wait," he said, wiggling his eyebrows.

She laughed and picked up her gear. "Letch."

Frank took her tote bag. "Let me carry this for you." He helped her down the steps, and they found a seat a few rows back from the front just as a group of teenagers started a rap number.

"I can tell I'm getting old," she whispered. "Rap just doesn't do it for me."

"Me, either. I can't even understand the words."

Next up was an elderly husband and wife banjo team who seemed very sweet, but their performance was just this side of terrible. Then Millie shyly took the stage.

From the first few words of "Summertime" until the last note died, Carrie wasn't sure that she breathed. Chill bumps covered her arms. Dear Lord, the woman was magnificent. She jumped to her feet and burst into applause.

Frank stood beside her. "Good, isn't she?"

"Good doesn't begin to describe it. She's spell-binding. I have no doubt that if she'd had the chance, Millie could have made it big-time. I wonder if she's content with her choice."

"Sometimes what seem to be choices," Frank said, "aren't really choices at all. Sometimes things are simply…" He shrugged.

"Fate?"

"For lack of a better word."

"Are you saying that you believe in karma?" she asked.

"It seems to be as good an explanation as any."

Barry Bledsoe joined them just then and the philosophical conversation halted. "I wanted to ask you two if you would do a duet I had in mind for the sixties. I want to feature two or three songs or dances or skits for each decade. Everybody will be on stage and the spotlight will focus on one act at a time."

"Sounds good," Carrie said. "What did you have in mind for us?"

"Sonny and Cher doing 'I Got You Babe.' Of course you're a better singer than Sonny ever was, Frank, but you can play it for laughs with funky costumes. Game?"

Frank looked at Carrie. "Any objections?"

"No, I don't mind. Maybe Kelly's employee can get music for us, and it shouldn't take too much practice."

"Great," Barry said. "I'm assigning your group to Patsy Hay. She's the girl in the red shirt down by the steps. Check scheduling with her. And Mick

O'Connor, the tall guy next to her, is in charge of the fifties, Carrie.''

After they talked with the assistant directors and got their instructions, it was almost noon. Frank said, ''I've got to be going. I promised the kids that we'd go riding after lunch. Thunder and Lightning haven't had much of a workout this week.''

''Thunder and Lightning?''

''The twins' ponies.''

''I didn't know you had horses.''

''It never came up,'' he said, flashing a lopsided smile. ''Say, what's this about you being a lawyer?''

''Nothing earth-shattering. I went to law school, took the bar exam. Passed.''

''And decided to go into genealogy? A bit of a leap, isn't it?''

*Tell him. This is the perfect opening.*

''Well,'' she said, ''that's not exactly—''

''Hey, Carrie!'' J.J. said as he approached grinning. ''You and Kelly were something else. You're one talented lady. Any more secrets you've been keeping from us?''

''One or two,'' she said, returning his grin. ''Women should always have a few secrets, don't you think,'' she asked, turning to Frank.

''I'm not big on secrets,'' Frank said. ''I'm an open and direct kind of guy myself.''

''’Scuse me for butting in,'' J.J. said, ''but Mary Beth wanted me to ask you what time we should come over to go riding. Katy hasn't talked about anything else in two days.''

''If you want a hot dog for lunch, come on now. If not, make it about one-thirty,'' Frank said.

"I'll pass on the hot dogs. We're having leftovers from the tearoom for lunch. See you later."

After J.J. left, Frank said, "You're welcome to have a hot dog with us, too, but I didn't figure that you would be interested in riding horses."

"And why is that?"

"You're a city girl."

"And city girls aren't interested in riding horses?" she asked sharply, feeling a little ticked that he'd stereotyped her.

"Hey." He threw up his hands in surrender. "I didn't mean to insult you. Do you ride?"

"I haven't been on a horse in a while, but I think I can manage to stay in a saddle."

"Then you're welcome to come out to my place and have a hot dog and go riding with us."

That wasn't the most enthusiastic invitation she'd ever received. She was tempted to say something snide, then thought better of it. "Thanks, but maybe I can make it another time. I have to be going." Feeling a bit stung, she turned and started up the aisle of the auditorium.

Frank caught up with her. "Say, that didn't come out exactly right. Let me start over. Carrie, I would like for you to come over and have hot dogs and potato chips with my family and me, and then go horseback riding. How about it?"

She hesitated.

"Pretty please? With sugar on it?"

She chuckled. "I think I'll pass on the hot dogs, but I'd like to go riding if it isn't an imposition."

"No imposition. Absolutely not. But I wish you'd reconsider lunch. Janey would be thrilled if you came."

"Thanks, but I have to change, and I have a couple of phone calls to make. I'll come at one-thirty."

"Great." He smiled. "I'll saddle Betsy for you."

Betsy sounded like a very old and gentle mare, but Carrie didn't comment.

Frank gave her directions to his place—as if she didn't know exactly where his property was—and they parted in the parking lot.

Was seeing so much of Frank wise? she wondered. Dating was one thing, but joining in family get-togethers was quite another. If she hadn't been so eager to go riding that her itch overrode her good sense, she would have said no. In fact, being mounted on a swaybacked nag wasn't her idea of a stimulating afternoon. She'd sooner stay in her room and read the mystery she'd gotten from the library.

No, that wasn't true. The day was too glorious to sit in a stuffy room reading.

When she reached her car, Carrie phoned Kelly at home. Not expecting her to answer, she was caught off guard when the voice said, "Dr. Martin."

"Hi, Kel. I figured you were still at the hospital delivering babies."

"Baby. Just one—a beautiful little girl. She was in a hurry to get here. I just walked in. What's up?"

They discussed practice schedules for a few moments, then Carrie said, "I need a favor."

"I owe you one. What do you need?"

"I need to find out why Wes Outlaw blocked an oil lease deal several years ago. I'm sure it was before you came here, but could you find out for me? Unobtrusively."

"I can try. When was this?"

Carrie told her all that she knew about the situation.

"There are a couple of people that I think I can ask about it. Unobtrusively. I'll get back to you in a day or two. Want to come over for potluck lunch?"

"Could I have a raincheck?"

"How about tomorrow?"

"Sorry, I'm going to play golf with Frank."

"Golf?"

"Sure. I love golf."

"Takes all kinds," Kelly said. "Well, if you'd rather go knock a ball around with the town hunk than have a chicken salad sandwich with me, so be it."

Carrie laughed and told Kelly goodbye.

THE MAILBOX beside the drive where she turned said simply Outlaw. Carrie pulled to a stop in front of the large white house shaded by tall pines, large oaks and a sweet gum or two. To the right was an orchard and to the left was a huge magnolia tree, and behind that, a barn. Flower beds were bright with yellow mums, and she suspected that in the spring, the azaleas and dogwoods would be beautiful. The house was reminiscent of an old Queen Anne Victorian with a deep wraparound porch adorned with hanging baskets of plants. As she climbed the steps she noticed there were several rocking chairs along the wall. And a swing. She loved porch swings.

She didn't have time to ring the bell before the door opened. "Hello," Frank said, eyeing her well-worn boots, jeans and long-sleeved plaid shirt. "You look like a regular cowgirl."

"My mother always said that choosing the right outfit was half the battle."

He laughed. "Come on in. Katy and the twins are

out back eager to go. J.J. and Mary Beth are helping Bud saddle the mounts.''

"I like your house," Carrie said as they walked down a wide entryway and through the family room at the back.

"Thanks. I've lived here all my life."

"All your life?"

"Yep. Except for when—except for a few years. And as a matter of fact, my dad was born here."

That sense of family history and permanence was an alien concept to Carrie. "So it belonged to your grandfather?"

Frank nodded. "It's been updated a few times since then. When my folks decided that they just rattled around in the place and decided to divide things up and move to town, I ended up with the house. It seemed logical at the time."

Carrie didn't mention that she was aware that his portion of the acreage was a bit less than that of his brothers and sister—to make up for the house she imagined.

The family room that they moved through was a big, homey place with a huge fireplace and oversize furniture, and she could see a modern kitchen to her left. This part looked as if it might have been added on or at least enlarged at some time. They went through French doors that led to a deck and a large swimming pool, then headed in the direction of the weathered red barn.

The twins and Katy sat atop a railing at the corral. Mary Beth was with them, and three ponies stood saddled and tied nearby. J.J. and a young man were saddling four other mounts—two solid-looking brown quarter horses and two paints.

Carrie greeted Mary Beth and the children.

"Daddy said you're going to ride Betsy," Janey said to Carrie. "She was my mommy's horse. My pony is named Lightning. That's her—the gray one." She pointed to a docile-looking pony.

"And mine is Thunder," Jimmy said.

"Mine is Ariel," Katy said. "I named her after the Little Mermaid."

"Great names," Carrie said to the kids, then turned her attention to the horses inside the corral.

When she looked closely at one of the paints, her breath caught. Loudly colored and spirited, it was a magnificent animal—reminded her of Calico, the horse she'd ridden and loved as a girl. Frank could ride poky Betsy. She intended to ride that one.

"I'm in love," Carrie said to Frank.

He hesitated for a couple of beats, then said, "Anybody I know?"

"The paint that J.J. is saddling."

"That's Betsy."

"*That's* Betsy."

"Yep."

"Why would anybody name a magnificent animal like that one...*Betsy* for goshsakes?"

"She was named when we got her. Calico Summer's Betsy. She hasn't been ridden much lately, and she seems a little fractious today. J.J. can ride her, and you can take one of the quarter horses."

"Over my dead body. I'd love to know her bloodlines."

"I have all the papers back at the house," Frank said.

Carrie merely nodded and went into the corral where J.J. was just tightening the cinch. "Hi, J.J. I've come to get acquainted with Betsy before we go for a ride.''

"Sure you want to ride her? She's pretty frisky. I wouldn't want you to get hurt.''

"I'm an experienced rider," Carrie told him. "I can handle her.''

J.J. hesitated, looking skeptical. Frank, who'd joined them, looked downright nervous.

Carrie ignored them both and began patting and talking to the horse, cooing the same words she'd always used with Calico. She knew immediately when she'd connected with the animal. The paint gave one last snort and toss of her head, then settled down.

"She just wants to run," Carrie said. "Which way do I go?''

"Anywhere in that direction," J.J. said, pointing south. "There's a path.''

"Wait and I'll come with you," Frank said.

But Carrie had already swung into the saddle and was headed out of the corral. Talk about déjà vu, it was like being sixteen and on Calico again. She touched Betsy's sides with her heels and they took off like the wind.

## Chapter Eleven

When Frank saw Carrie take off lickety-split, it scared the devil out of him. He sprang into Apache's saddle, yelled, "Watch the kids," and took out after her.

He couldn't catch her.

When he finally drew within sight, he could see that she was bent low over Betsy's neck—probably holding on for dear life and frightened to death. Urging Apache faster, he closed the gap until he could see that Carrie wasn't on a runaway—or frightened.

She was laughing, and she rode as if she were born in a saddle. He wanted to break her neck.

Carrie slowed, and Frank drew up beside her. She was still laughing.

"You scared the hell out of me," he bellowed.

Sobering instantly, she looked at him as if he were a frog in a punch bowl. "Who stepped on your tail, Your Honor?" She turned Betsy and walked her through a pasture full of yellow wildflowers.

He followed and caught up with her. "I'm sorry. I thought that Betsy had run away with you and you were in trouble. I must have aged ten years when I saw you shoot off."

Looking amused, she patted Betsy's neck. "I'll

have you know that I was a junior barrel racing champion for three years running. And on a paint that could be a twin of this one. I lost her a few years ago, and it broke my heart."

"You're a great rider," he said as they walked the horses through the pasture. "You look like you grew up in the saddle."

"Except for occasional pony rides at the fair, I didn't get on a horse until I was fourteen and went to live on my uncle's ranch. Then you couldn't get me off one. Calico was just over a year old when I arrived, and we sort of grew up together."

"Calico?"

"My horse. Windwood's Calico Spring. She had a foal named Calico Summer Storm that paid my way through law school."

"How so?"

"His sire was a champion, and he won a bunch of awards as well. A fellow in Louisiana was eager to have him. Turned out that a rancher in Dallas wanted him, too. They got into a bidding war, and he brought big bucks."

"Who got him?" Frank asked.

"The man from Louisiana. When I heard Betsy's name, I wondered if she might have been from the same line. Of course Calico is a common name for piebalds."

"It might be a possibility. I bought Betsy through a breeder in Shreveport. We can check it out."

"Wouldn't that be something if they were related? She's such a beauty." Betsy tossed her head as if agreeing. Carrie smiled and patted the horse's neck. "She knows she's special. Would you consider selling her to me?"

Frank shook his head. "Sorry, I couldn't. She... well, she's not for sale."

"I understand. Janey said she was your wife's horse."

"Yes. I'd just bought her for Susan's birthday the week before she...was killed. Susan only rode her once." The mention of Susan's name brought back painful memories as it always did. Susan hadn't been as thrilled by the gift of a horse as he figured she might be. Oh, she was gracious about it, but he could see the disappointment in her eyes. He could kick himself all over again when he thought about it.

"Betsy's not for sale," Frank said, "but you're welcome to come and ride her as often as you like while you're here."

"Don't offer that or I'll be here every day."

"That's okay. As you can tell, she'd love the exercise."

The kids came riding up on their ponies, with Mary Beth and J.J. following.

"Did Daddy save you?" Janey asked.

Frank laughed. "Carrie didn't need saving. Seems that she's a champion barrel racer."

"What's a barrel racer?" Jimmy asked.

"It's those ladies that run their horses around those barrels at the rodeo," Janey informed him.

"They ride really, really fast," Katy said.

"Carrie, can you teach me to race barrels?" Janey asked.

"Me, too," Katy said.

"I think you might be a little bit young yet. Maybe in a couple of years."

"Or ten," Mary Beth added.

"We're going to where Uncle J.J. is building his house," Janey said.

"And it's going to be Mommy's and my house, too," Katy said. "Me and Janey and Jimmy are gonna be neighbors when we get married and the house is finished."

"When you and Janey and Jimmy get married?" Carrie asked.

Katy giggled. "No. When J.J. and Mommy and me get married at Christmas. Come on, let's go see." She nudged the sides of her pony and turned back to the trail.

Mary Beth and J.J. fell in behind them, and Carrie and Frank brought up the rear.

CARRIE LOVED the house J.J. was building, and obviously Mary Beth loved it, too. She proudly showed off the four bedrooms and three baths that were ready for painting. They discussed colors and light fixtures and carpet as they moved through the airy rooms, and their voices echoed in the big empty space.

The children caught on to the weird sounds they could make by shouting. Soon they were running through the rooms shrieking and laughing and getting totally out of hand.

"Hey, guys," Frank said, "cut it out."

They were quiet for about thirty seconds, then they started again. Mary Beth snagged Katy as she ran through, held her fingers to her lips and shook her head. Katy stood quietly by her mother looking sheepish. Janey and Jimmy got wilder and wilder until Carrie was tempted to say something herself. Their shrieking was at headache level.

"Janey! Jimmy!" Frank said. "Outside for a time-out."

The noise stopped instantly. He followed them downstairs, and then Carrie could hear Janey begin to whine and wail.

"Come on, sweet pea," J.J. said to Katy. "Let's go talk about where you want the bookshelves in your room."

"Kids," Mary Beth said. "Sometimes they have more energy than they know what to do with."

"I have to admire good parents. I'm certainly not cut out for the job," Carrie said.

Mary Beth laughed. "There are days I think the same thing, but it grows on you. I can't imagine life without Katy."

They went downstairs and talked about kitchen amenities and the advantages of various types of countertops—which bored Carrie to no end. Even at home in her town house, she spent as little time as possible in the kitchen. A cook she was not.

When it was time to leave they went outside and found Frank sitting on the steps. The twins were sitting one on each end of the long plantation porch. Jimmy looked contrite. Janey looked sullen.

Spotting Carrie, Frank shrugged as if to apologize. He went first to Jimmy and spoke quietly. Jimmy nodded and Frank hugged him and gave him a playful swat toward the horses. He then spoke to Janey, whose bottom lip continued to jut out. She shook her head defiantly. He continued to talk until finally she nodded as well. He hugged her, too. Janey seemed unenthusiastic in her response and shot Carrie a glare over Frank's shoulder and stuck out her tongue. The little stinker didn't seem at all contrite as she trudged toward her pony.

"Sorry," Frank said to Carrie. "Sometimes they can get a bit rambunctious. I think they're tired. Are you ready to head back or would you like to ride a while longer?"

She glanced at her watch. "Let's go back. It's been fun, but I have some work yet to do."

They rode back to the corral, and as soon as the horses were tended to, Janey, who was still sulking and hadn't said a word to anybody, ran into the house.

"Janey seems very upset," Carrie said to Frank. "What did you say to her? No, strike that. It's none of my business."

"No big deal. I simply told her that her behavior wasn't very ladylike and that I was ashamed of her for acting so inconsiderately, especially in front of a guest. I think that she was embarrassed. Janey is usually pretty well behaved, thank goodness, because she doesn't take discipline well. She's one of those kids who's five going on forty."

Carrie didn't mention Janey's rude behavior behind his back. She figured that Janey blamed "the guest" for her being chastised by her father, and that was probably the reason for the glare and the tongue. She'd felt the same way herself a few times. Being a kid and powerless was tough.

Carrie considered offering to talk to Janey, but she didn't want to interfere. Besides, he knew a lot more about kids that she did. She was certainly no expert.

She thanked Frank for the ride, and after they set a time for their game on Sunday, she left.

BACK IN HER ROOM at the Twilight Inn, Carrie called Kelly to see if she was free for dinner. Luckily she had no plans, so the two of them drove over to Travis Lake for Chinese.

Kelly paused over her spring roll and said, "It's pretty sad when two reasonably attractive, intelligent and charming women are reduced to eating with each other on a Saturday night."

"I don't know," Carrie said. "I've had worse dates. At least you don't have bad breath."

Kelly chuckled. "Tell me that after I've eaten the garlic chicken."

"Have you been able to find out anything about why the Outlaws wrecked the last oil lease deal?"

"I talked to my nurse about it. Elaine grew up here and knows everything and everybody. She vaguely remembers the situation. She said it wasn't actually Wes who was so much opposed to it, but she doesn't recall the details. Elaine said that her uncle would know. She was going to find out this weekend and let me know on Monday."

"I hope she'll be discreet," Carrie said.

"Not to worry. Trust me, she knows how to handle things, and she'll report all the skinny on the Outlaws and their part in that old deal that fell through. And speaking of Outlaws, why aren't you out with Frank tonight?"

"In the first place, he didn't ask me. I think he wanted to spend the evening with his kids."

"Jimmy and Janey are sweethearts. They've had a tough time. And Frank's had it rough since Susan died. Not only has he had to deal with his own grief, but also he's had to be both mother and father to the twins."

"Our assistant director for the Follies wants to

meet with the whole fifties group on Monday evening at seven-thirty,'' Carrie said as she spooned rice onto her plate. ''Is that okay with you?''

''Sure. I'll make my rounds early. Where are we meeting?''

''At the auditorium. Then individual rehearsals will be in unit two at the Inn. Mary Beth has graciously loaned it to the various groups who need a place to practice.''

Kelly's fork poised midway to her mouth, and a shocked expression flashed over her face.

''What's wrong?'' Carrie asked, starting to turn and glance in the direction of Kelly's stare.

''Don't turn around!'' Kelly whispered, but of course Carrie did.

Kelly smiled broadly and waved to a couple across the room. The man nodded and ducked his head. The blond woman with him didn't respond at all.

''Who's that?'' Carrie asked.

''My neurologist friend. No wonder I haven't heard from him lately. Looks like he's found a replacement for me.''

''Men can be such jerks. Well, don't worry about it. From what I can tell he wasn't any great loss.''

''Amen. Pass the soy sauce.''

''DADDY, can we go riding again today?'' Jimmy asked during Sunday dinner.

''You'll have to ask Pawpaw when he gets here,'' Frank said. ''I'm going to play golf this afternoon.''

''Can we go?'' Janey asked. ''I like golf.''

''This isn't the miniature kind, punkin'. This is the grown-up kind. It would be pretty boring for you.''

''Are you going with Uncle J.J.?'' Janey asked.

"No, I'm going with Carrie Campbell."

"I don't think she likes me," Janey said. "I was very, very bad yesterday."

"You weren't bad, Janey. You just forgot your manners for a while. I know you won't do that again."

"May I be excused?" Jimmy said, already lifting his plate to take it to the kitchen.

"You may," Frank said. "Change your clothes before you go outside."

"Yes, sir."

"Daddy," Janey said, "do you like Carrie a lot?"

"She's a very nice lady."

"Would you 'pologize to her for me? Tell her I'm very, very, very sorry for being bad?"

"I'll tell her that you were sorry for forgetting your manners. Okay?"

"Just tell her the other. Please?"

Since it seemed important to her, Frank agreed to tell Carrie Janey's exact words, and the two of them cleared the table.

After Frank changed into his golf clothes and loaded his clubs and bag into the trunk, he remembered that he was going to look up Betsy's lineage. Since he still had a few minutes before he had to pick up Carrie, he went into his study and found the papers.

There, two generations back was Calico's Summer Storm, the horse Carrie had said paid her way through law school. He shook his head. Amazing coincidence. Carrie would be thrilled to know that Betsy was a descendant of her beloved horse. He really ought to sell Betsy to her. It wasn't as if Susan had been attached to the paint.

But he simply couldn't get rid of anything that was Susan's. All her clothes were still packed away in boxes in the attic, and many of her belongings were still in drawers in their bedroom. His mother had offered to go through things and give Susan's stuff to charity, but he couldn't bring himself to let go of it. Opening one of Susan's drawers and smelling the lingering scent of her distinctive sachets was the last little bit of her he had left. Her clothes would have been hanging in the closet as well if he and the twins hadn't moved into this house with his folks after she died.

The scents were fading, and now and then Susan's face seemed a little blurry in his memory. That bothered him. He picked up a photograph from his desk. It was a family picture taken only a few weeks before she died. The twins had grown and changed remarkably since that time. Even he looked different—a few more gray hairs and a few pounds—but Susan was frozen in time forever, smiling and young.

He wondered if Susan would have liked Carrie. Probably so. Susan liked almost everybody.

Frank replaced the photo and left the house before the guilt feelings started to gnaw on him again. He was looking forward to a lively game of golf.

"THAT WAS GREAT," Carrie said as they rode back to the clubhouse in the cart. "Sorry I'm a little rusty."

"Rusty?" Frank said. "If you'd been any more up on your game, you'd have whipped me good."

"I doubt that. You're no slouch. I really enjoyed playing with you this afternoon. I've missed being out on the course."

"Worked up an appetite?" Frank asked as they pulled up in the lot beside his car.

"You betcha. I'll meet you back here in twenty minutes."

They moved the clubs from the cart to his car, and she hurried to the women's locker room to shower and change. She hadn't just been polite when she told Frank how much she had enjoyed herself. He was a terrific player, and she'd given it everything she had trying to beat him—or at least not embarrass herself. He'd beaten her by six strokes. True, she wasn't as familiar with the course as he was, but she doubted that she could have done much better. She had a sneaky feeling that, despite his gentlemanly ways and laid-back style, Frank was playing for blood, too. She was beginning to realize that he was a lot tougher and more competitive than one would first assume.

She showered and changed quickly into black pants and a mauve cotton sweater set. After a few makeup repairs, she grabbed her bag and made it to the parking lot just about on time.

Frank was waiting. "You made it with twenty-nine seconds to spare. I'm surprised."

"Why? I'm *always* prompt."

"I suppose it's hard to understand how you can make yourself so beautiful in such a short time. Must be natural."

"Whoa. Are you smooth or what?" Even though she teased, she was enormously pleased by his compliment.

He took her bag and helped her into the car. When he climbed behind the wheel, he said, "Is Chinese okay?"

She didn't tell him that was what she'd had the night before. "I adore Chinese."

They ended up at the same restaurant. Luckily, the food there was great, and she sampled a different dish that evening. A couple of times, Carrie glanced up from her food to find him staring at her strangely. The second time it happened, she said, "Why are you looking at me like that? Do I have spinach in my teeth or something?"

He smiled and shook his head. "Your teeth are perfect. In fact, everything about you is just about perfect. I was wishing that we were someplace more private—someplace where I could take you into my arms and kiss you."

"Kiss me?"

"And more."

Warmth raced over her, and she felt a throbbing low in her body. She tried to say something, but nothing came out of her mouth.

"Want to go to a movie and make out in the balcony?" he asked.

"Not when I have a perfectly private motel room."

"And a town full of people with stopwatches. Want some dessert?"

She shook her head. He signaled for the check.

While Frank signed the charge ticket, Carrie broke open her fortune cookie and pulled out the little paper.

"What does it say?" he asked.

"It says, 'You are charming, intelligent and an excellent golfer who will go far in the world.'"

Frank chuckled and grabbed for the slip. "'Fortune favors the brave,'" he read. "Are you brave?"

"No guts, no glory. I once considered becoming a matador."

"But you chickened out?"

"Nope. Waving a cape at a bull wasn't the problem. I decided that I couldn't bring myself to skewer the poor thing simply for entertainment. What does yours say?"

He broke open his fortune cookie and read it aloud. "'Beware the fury of a patient man.' This must belong to somebody else. I don't know any patient men—except maybe Jacob Appleberry, and he's ninety-three. If he got furious he'd probably have a heart attack."

"You strike me as a patient man."

"Me? Nah. It's all a facade. Ready to go?"

She nodded, and they left. Carrie wasn't nearly as brave as she'd claimed. If she were really brave, she'd suggest that they drive to the nearest motel and rent a room.

Apparently Frank's thoughts were running along the same track. He didn't take the usual route home to Naconiche. Instead he took a more deserted route along the shore of the lake the town was named for.

"Where are we going?" Carrie asked.

"Somewhere I haven't been in years."

"And where is that?"

"Parking. Mind?"

"I don't think I've done that since I've been an adult."

He chuckled. "Me, either, but I'm getting desperate to kiss you, to…"

"To…" she asked playfully.

"To do anything you want. The sky's the limit."

A thrill went through her as he pulled into a secluded area by a picnic table and stopped. He let down the windows and turned off the engine. The area was thickly wooded and dark now with the car lights off. Only a half-moon, a sky full of stars and a few distant flickers across the water illuminated the night.

The air was pleasantly cool and filled with the scent of pine trees and damp shore. Tree frogs chirred their continuous song, and now and then there was a splash in the water.

"Looks like this place is still used for the same purpose after all these years," Frank said, nodding to another car barely visible through the trees to the left.

Maybe it was a sense of the risk involved or maybe it was simply the anticipation of being intimate with this incredibly sexy man or maybe it was because she had been celibate for so long—or maybe all of the above—but she was already becoming aroused, and they were still in their seat belts.

She heard the click of his seat belt opening and the clunk of the steering wheel being raised. For a moment she seemed paralyzed, but her heart was going ninety miles an hour. Then he reached over and pushed the latch on her seat belt. It retracted with a quick *zippp, thunk,* and she felt almost naked.

He scooted across the seat and scooped her into his arms. "I've been aching to do this all day," he whispered. His mouth, warm and urgent, covered hers, and his tongue probed between her lips.

Her arms went around him, and she returned the kiss just as urgently. His hands stroked her back, slipped under her sweater and cupped her breasts. He murmured against her ear and kissed the side of her neck as he deftly unsnapped her bra.

"I want to taste you, Carrie," he said, pushing up

her sweater. "Desperately. I dream about tasting you."

His lips went to her breasts, and she went wild. Threading her fingers through his hair, she pulled his mouth closer to her and arched toward the exquisite feel of his tongue and teeth and lips, moaning as her arousal grew, whispering his name to urge him on.

There was a sharp knock on the car door, and Frank instantly froze. Carrie sobered as well. Over Frank's shoulder, she could only see a figure standing outside the car. Panicked, her thoughts flashed over every possibility from a policeman to a deranged serial killer with a chainsaw.

"Excuse me," a young male voice said.

Frank shielded Carrie while he pulled down her sweater, then he straightened and turned to the person outside.

"Oh, excuse me, sir. I didn't know…oh, God," he said to Frank, the sound of alarm raising his voice.

"What do you want?" Frank asked sharply.

"Oh, God, this is awful, sir. Just awful. My car won't start and Michelle is supposed to be home, and oh, God, my dad's gonna kill me."

"Get Michelle," Frank said. "I'll drive you home."

"Thank you, sir." The teenager dashed off.

"Frank, do you think it's wise to pick up strangers?"

"They're not strangers. They're from Naconiche. Kevin's father is the minister of the First Baptist Church, and Michelle is the daughter of the bank president."

Carrie tried hard not to laugh as she straightened her clothes, but a snort escaped anyhow. "Curses."

Frank didn't add "foiled again." He just shook his head. "This is getting old." Apparently he didn't see the humor in the situation.

When the two teenagers climbed quietly into the back seat, Frank turned around and said to them, "Guys, I won't tell if you won't tell."

# Chapter Twelve

Word must have spread fast because two of the women in the county clerk's office took one look at Carrie that Monday morning and giggled.

Carrie almost giggled herself. It *was* pretty funny—even if Frank was being a bear about the incident at the lake. People must have been giving him grief all morning.

"I may never live this down," he said as they drove to lunch. "Those two kids had better not show up in my court anytime in the next twenty years. If I weren't a man of my word, I'd call the preacher and the bank president and give them an earful."

Everybody in the place grinned at them when Carrie and Frank walked into the Twilight Tearoom for lunch. And wouldn't you know? The only empty seats in the place were the three at J.J.'s table.

"We'll wait," Frank said to Florence Russo, Dixie's mother-in-law, who was acting as hostess that day.

"It may be a while until a table is free," Florence said, "and J.J. told me he was saving a place for y'all."

About that time, J.J. stood up and waved broadly

to them. Only a blind person could have missed his gesture. Carrie discreetly covered her laughter with a cough and a fist to her mouth.

Frank frowned. "We might as well get this over with." With a look of grim determination, he grabbed her elbow and guided her to the table. After he'd seated her, Frank glared at J.J. "I don't want to hear one word out of you, little brother."

J.J. looked up, his expression as innocent as a cherub's. "About what? I don't know what you're talking about."

"Like hell you don't. Just keep your yap shut."

"Could I at least order my lunch?"

"If you'll confine your remarks to the items on the menu."

"Fair enough," J.J. said. "I see they have fish today. You like fish, don't you, Frank?"

He shrugged. "Pretty well."

"I thought you might," J.J. said, a mischievous gleam in his eye, "since I heard you went fishing last night over at Travis Lake." He reared back in his chair, and a huge grin spread over his face. "Catch anything?"

Suddenly J.J.'s chair tipped back too far, and the sheriff and his chair crashed to the floor like a shot. The place grew quiet enough to hear a mouse cough. Not a fork scraped a plate as everybody stopped to stare at the commotion.

Frank calmly leaned over and looked down at his brother sprawled on his back with his legs in the air. "You hurt yourself, J.J.?"

"Did you do that?" Carrie whispered.

"Nah. He's always been clumsy. J.J., did you hurt yourself?"

"I'm fine, big brother." J.J. stood, righted his chair, dusted his pants and sat back down.

"Just remember before you shoot your mouth off again," Frank said quietly, "that I can still take you any day of the week. I think you owe Carrie an apology."

J.J. sobered. "You're right. Carrie, I'm sorry if I embarrassed you. All the Outlaw boys are so used to hoorahing one another that sometimes we forget our manners."

"Don't worry about me," Carrie said. "I've got a thick skin. I grew up around a profession that carried on some pretty tough razzing. And as a matter of fact, I think the whole thing is a hoot."

"Yes, but you don't have to live here," Frank said. "J.J., is there anybody in town who doesn't know about last night at the lake?"

"Oh, a couple of people over at the hospital. But they're in a coma." J.J. snorted and ducked his head to hide his mirth.

Frank groaned. "Maybe folks will find something else to talk about in a day or two."

The waitress came to the table with glasses of raspberry tea. "What can I get for y'all today?"

They ordered lunch, and the food was delicious as usual. J.J. didn't do any more teasing, and their conversation turned to the Fall Follies. It seemed that each decade was meeting at fifteen-minute intervals that evening to block out their part in the show and receive practice materials.

"Mama said we're supposed to be there at seven," J.J. said as he rose. "Excuse me, but I want to see Mary Beth before I go back to the office."

After J.J. left, Frank asked, "Want me to pick you up tonight?"

"Tell you what," Carrie said. "How about I pick *you* up instead?"

Frank raised his eyebrows slightly. "That might work."

THAT EVENING Carrie was sitting in the back of the high school auditorium reading a book when Kelly slipped in beside her.

"You all alone?" Kelly asked.

"Yes," Carrie said. "Frank's backstage doing something. You're early."

"Wonder of wonders, I don't have a single patient in the hospital, so I didn't have to make rounds. I've been trying to find time all day to call you, but it's been hectic. Elaine found out about you-know-what," Kelly whispered.

"Elaine?"

"My nurse. You remember she was going to talk to her uncle about the old oil deal."

"Right," Carrie said. "What did she learn?"

"Well, according to her uncle, although Wes Outlaw took the blame for ruining the deal and talked some others into refusing to lease their land as well, he wasn't the big problem. Seems that the problem was really Clyde Burrows and his brother Walter."

"Walter?"

"Yes, he was Vernon's father, the one that owns the land that I got a part of. Walter died a few years ago in a tractor accident, and his land went to his son. Anyhow, Walter wanted to lease his land to the oil company, but Clyde refused to even talk to the landman. Threatened to shoot him if he set foot on his property. He also told his brother Walter that he'd unload a wad of buckshot in his britches and burn down his house if he tried to lease his land to them.''

"Good Lord. Would he have done it?'' Carrie asked.

"According to Elaine's uncle he would have. They say he's crazy mean and a crack shot. He lives like a recluse in a cabin with a bunch of dogs. He only comes to town occasionally for supplies. Don't tell me that you want to lease his property.''

Carrie made a face. "Yeah, I do. Why did people think Wes Outlaw was the problem?''

"I think Wes knew that without the big tract that Clyde owns, the oil company wouldn't want any of the land, so to keep peace, he talked down the deal. When Wes told the landman that his property wasn't for lease, either, the company gave up and pulled out. I don't know any more specifics.''

"Sounds like I'd better talk to Wes and the Burrows men pretty soon.''

"Just be careful that you don't get shot,'' Kelly said. "Have you told Frank about your being a landman yet?''

"Not yet. I was waiting to hear from you,'' Carrie said. "Looks like they're ready for our decade on the stage.''

They went down front and waved to Mary Beth, Dixie and Ellen who were just coming off the stage with the rest of the last group. She and Kelly joined a bunch assembled on stage while Mick, their assistant director, blocked out the fifties segment.

Carrie was concerned about costume changes between her two numbers, but the assistant directors worked things out so that the "Diamonds'' number would be first and they would be positioned stage right near the dressing rooms. With a little planning, there would be plenty of time for a change before she had to turn into Cher.

Kelly left, and Frank joined Carrie on stage to hear the same instructions for the sixties performers. Their person had copies of the words to "I Got You Babe" as well as a cassette of the music.

"Have you ever seen Sonny and Cher do this?" Frank asked as they left the auditorium.

"I'm a little too young. I wasn't even born when they held Woodstock, but I've seen bits and pieces of tapes here and there."

"It's before my time, too, but I happened to catch a bio of Sonny on TV the other night and recorded it. There were several clips of them singing this song, both early in their careers and then later on. I thought you might like to see it one night."

"That would be great."

"Want to stop somewhere for coffee?" Frank asked as he held open the door for her.

She smiled slowly. "I have coffee at my place. I even have…cake."

"You baked?"

"Defrosted."

He laughed. "You're on."

On the way back to the inn, her heart started doing that flamenco number again. She hoped he was prepared this time. But just in case he wasn't, she'd driven over to Lake Travis and stocked up on a variety of protective devices. She was more than ready.

But the powers that be weren't cooperating. When Carrie pulled into the drive there must have been a dozen cars parked in the lot at the tearoom, and the lights were on in both the tearoom and in unit two.

"Oops," Carrie said, stopping in front of her room. "I forgot that Monday is aerobics night."

"I thought Thursday was aerobics night," Frank said, clearly irritated.

"It is. Monday and Thursday. Want to chance it?"

About that time the door to unit two opened and women began coming out.

An older woman headed their way, and Frank groaned. "That's Mabel Fortney, the cashier at the tearoom. She's the worst gossip in fourteen counties."

"Yoo-hoo!" Mabel cried, waving.

"I'll handle her," Carrie mumbled out of the side of her mouth. She got out of the car and waved to Mabel. "How are you this evening?"

"Just fine. We missed you at aerobics class." Mabel smiled and glanced slyly at Frank. "But I can see that you had more important things to do."

"Frank and I are in a number together in the Fall Follies. We've been down at the high school, and I'm giving him a lift home. We just stopped by to pick up a book I'm loaning him." Carrie fluttered her fingers and went into her room.

Good thing she actually picked up a paperback she'd bought at the grocery store, for when Carrie came out of her room, Mabel was standing beside the car talking to Frank.

Carrie got into the car, handed Frank the book and said, "Bye, Mabel. I've got to get Frank home before he turns into a pumpkin."

Mabel tittered, and Frank shot Carrie a look that clearly said he wanted to strangle somebody. Carrie clenched her teeth to keep from laughing as she pulled away.

"Old biddy!" Frank mumbled.

"She's not. Mabel's a sweetheart."

"Right now I'm not feeling very kindly toward her. I guess we'll have to revert to plan B."

"What's plan B?" she asked.

"I go home and take a cold shower."

So much for their romantic tryst.

Small town mentality could be a real pain in the posterior.

ON TUESDAY MORNING, Carrie drove over to Bowen, seat of the neighboring county to the east. A small section of the land she wanted to lease was in the next county. Just about finished with her research in Naconiche County, she was ready to start hustling property owners to sign on the dotted line. She told herself that it would be easier to locate the landowners in Bowen County and get them out of the way first. She didn't kid herself that it also delayed having to come clean with Frank and the others about her real purpose for coming to town.

She had meant to tell Frank the night before, but when she'd pulled up in front of his house to drop him off, there hadn't even been an opportunity for a good-night kiss. The twins had come bounding out in their pajamas to exclaim that the cat had delivered kittens. Six of them.

Carrie parked in front of the Bowen County courthouse and went inside. The building didn't have the charm of the one in Naconiche. It was a modern box with lots of windows. But it also had a whiz of a computer system. This would be a piece of cake.

She had lunch at a greasy spoon even worse than the City Grill. As she was leaving the place, she spotted a large music store two doors down and went inside to see if she could find a CD of Sonny and Cher. They had one copy of ''The Best of'' songs, and Carrie bought it. She could sing along while she drove and learn the words of the Follies' number.

By midafternoon Carrie had all the data she needed. Luckily the parcel she was interested in was owned by only two men. That made leasing simple.

Unfortunately, one was having his gallbladder removed and the other, a packing plant owner, was out of town until Thursday. She tried to see to the guy in the hospital, but his wife said he was still too groggy to talk. By the time she left the hospital it was after five o'clock, and she was tired and thirsty. On her way out of town, with the top down and singing loudly with Sonny and Cher, she spotted a convenience store and pulled in. A cold cola would be wonderful. And maybe a candy bar. She hadn't eaten much of that gross lunch.

Carrie had just turned off the engine when she heard an awful commotion inside the store—shouting and what sounded like gunshots. *Get gone!* she told herself.

She started the car and was shoving the gear in Reverse when the door opened and a young man came running from the store. He vaulted into her convertible and stuck a gun in her side. She almost wet herself.

''Drive!'' he yelled over the whine of Sonny on the CD.

She drove. Pedal to the metal, she peeled away

from the store, almost colliding with a blue pickup pulling in.

"Calm down," she told the kid, who, despite his attempt at a mustache, couldn't have been more than sixteen or seventeen. He was wild-eyed and shaking. "Just calm down. Nobody needs to get hurt."

She reached to turn off the CD, and he yelled, "Keep both hands on the wheel."

Carrie left Sonny and Cher singing loudly and told herself to keep cool so she could think of a way to get out of this, but her adrenaline was already a quart high and keeping cool was out of the question. The kid was scared and very nervous and, from the looks of the paper sack clutched in his left hand, had just robbed that store. He might have even shot somebody already, so shooting her wouldn't make things any worse for him.

"My name is Carrie. What's yours?"

"This ain't no tea party, lady. Shut up and keep driving. Faster."

She was already doing eighty. Where was a cop when you needed one? She prayed that one would appear out of the blue.

"Tell you what," she said. "I'll call you Joe. I knew a boy in high school named Joe, and you remind me of him." Trying to personalize things always worked in situations like this on TV.

"My name ain't Joe. It's H…Hank."

Hearing another faint whine in between Sonny's, she thought her prayer had been answered and glanced in the rearview mirror hoping to see flashing lights coming to the rescue.

Nothing but pavement and a lone pickup truck.

But the whine grew louder.

There it was! Coming toward them, siren wailing and red-and-blue lights flashing, was a cop car. Praise be.

The kid let out a string of oaths that would have done a driller proud. Carrie wanted to honk her horn and wave, but she kept her hands on the wheel and tried mental telepathy instead.

But damn! The brown car roared right past.

"Turn right at the next road," Hank shouted. He poked her side with the gun, glanced over his shoulder and cursed some more. "Right there! Right there!"

Carrie slammed on her brakes and fishtailed onto the dirt road, sending up a plume of dust.

"Now, floorboard it. Go! Go!"

She stomped the accelerator and roared down the winding road.

Oh, God, was he going to shoot her and steal her car? If she slammed on her brakes, he might crack his head and knock himself out. Even if he didn't, she might be able to wrestle the gun from him. She wasn't going down without a fight.

"Stop here! Around that next curve! Stop and let me out. Then you keep going, lady. Drive like the devil is on your tail."

Carrie didn't argue. She screeched to a stop; the kid jumped from the car and ran through a thick stand of trees. He stopped only long enough to turn and fire one shot at her.

Ducking low, she peeled out, slinging gravel and dirt as she raced away. Totally unfamiliar with the area, she had no idea where she was going. Coming to a Y, she hesitated briefly, then took the left angle, hoping she'd run across some sign of civilization. But she didn't see a house or a cow or anything except woods that got thicker and thicker. It was growing dark, and the ruts of the dirt road she was on got deeper and deeper and more washed out. She slowed and bounced along, bottoming out a couple of times. And then the road petered out at a steep riverbank. Good thing she'd been going slow or she would have sailed right over.

She stopped, got out and peered over the bank at the murky water below. Going to the left at that Y had been a bad choice. She walked around for a minute or two, taking deep breaths to calm herself, then she got back into the car, backed up and turned around. Surely by now Hank, or whatever his name was, would be long gone, and it would be safe for her to retrace her route back to the highway and find a cop of some kind.

What was she thinking? She popped her forehead with the heel of her hand, then reached for her cell phone in her bag.

But her bag was gone.

She stopped and looked all over the car for it. No bag.

She stood in the middle of the road with her hands on her hips and turned the air blue. That little snot had stolen her purse!

Her cash, her credit cards, her phone—everything was gone.

Furious, Carrie got into her car and bumped back down the cow path headed for a phone.

Not half a mile along, she spotted a brown vehicle blocking the road. Its lights were flashing, and a big shield that said Deputy Sheriff adorned the door.

Her shoulders sagged with relief.

She pulled to a stop and leaned her head against the wheel, thankful that her ordeal was over.

"Keep your hands where I can see them," a bullhorn echoed, "and get out of the car."

Carrie looked around, then realized that meant her. She opened the door, got out and raised her hands.

A plump kid in a cowboy hat and with a badge pinned to his chest approached with the bullhorn and a drawn gun. "That goes for your partner, too."

"I don't have a partner. There's only me. Boy, am I glad to—"

"Put your hands on the hood," the bullhorn blared, "and spread your legs."

"I beg your pardon!" Carrie said indignantly.

"Do it!" He waved the gun.

This kid looked wilder than Hank. She put her hands on the hood and spread her legs.

## Chapter Thirteen

"Carrie?"

Glancing up from her seat in the cell, she saw Frank standing on the other side of the bars. He looked like a grim angel. Despite being humiliated out of her mind that he should find her like this, she'd never been so happy to see anyone in her life. It was two o'clock in the morning, and she'd been through eight or nine hours of pure hell.

She jumped up. "Frank! How did you know I was here?"

"J.J. called me as soon as he found out about it. What the devil happened?"

"I just stopped to get a Coke. Before I could get out of the car, a kid ran from the convenience store, jumped in my car, stuck a gun in my ribs and told me to drive. What would you do? He bailed out along some pig trail with my bag. I don't have any identification or any money. These yahoos are convinced that I'm Hank's accomplice."

"Who's Hank?"

"The robber. Only I don't know if that's his real name. I'm a *victim* here. I've tried my very best to be cooperative. I told them my name. I explained my business in town. But without my identification, I can't even prove that my car belongs to me. I can't get hold of my uncle or my cousin, and when they didn't believe a word I said, I lost my temper. I told them that I was a lawyer and that I was going to sue everybody in this place…and a few other uncomplimentary things.

"After they stuck me in here, I begged them to call the sheriff in Naconiche to vouch for me. I was afraid they wouldn't."

"Somebody called J.J. less than an hour ago," Frank said. "I got here as quickly as I could. Let me go make arrangements, then we'll get your stuff and go home."

"What stuff?" she asked, her voice rising an octave. "I don't have any stuff." She plucked at the legs of her pants. "All I have is what I'm wearing. Hank stole my bag, and my car has been impounded until they can fingerprint it. And God knows when this bunch of ignorant redneck jerks will get around to doing that!"

"Just calm down, Carrie," Frank said. "I'll be right back."

True to his word, Frank was back in a few minutes with the jailer.

"I'm real sorry about this, Judge," the jailer said as he unlocked the cell. "Just as sorry as I can be."

"Why are you apologizing to *him?*" Carrie said as she glared at the man. "*I'm* the one you should be apologizing to. *I'm* the one you screwed up and threw in jail. Just wait. I—"

Frank grabbed her elbow. "Let's go, Carrie." He steered her from the jail and out the door. He didn't say another word until they were on the highway back to Naconiche.

"The deputy mentioned that you told them you were a landman and had come to the area to secure oil leases for your company," Frank said quietly. Too quietly.

A horrible sinking feeling came over Carrie, and she closed her eyes. She'd waited too long to tell him the truth; she hadn't wanted him to find out like this.

"Is it true?" he asked.

"Yes, but I can explain."

"How do you explain lying?"

"I didn't lie," she said. "Not exactly. I simply avoided telling the entire truth. Uncle Tuck asked me to keep quiet about my business until I had done the research and was ready to start leasing property."

"Who is Uncle Tuck?"

"Tucker Campbell, president of Campbell Oil Exploration and Development. Frank, the oil business is extremely competitive, and if the wrong people found out I was leasing in the area, it could be disastrous."

"For whom?"

"For everybody. I'd planned to tell you about being a landman last night, but...well, things came up."

His silence said that he didn't buy it.

"It's true."

"Were you going to tell me before or after we went to bed together?"

"That's a low blow."

"Is it? Tell me, is any Outlaw land included in the property you want to lease?"

"Yes, but—"

"Don't say anymore, Carrie. Not now."

"But—"

"Not now, I said. I'm not in the mood to hear it."

She knew that trying to explain now would be dumb. She shut up. Not another word passed between them until he drove up to the front of her room and stopped.

"Good night," he said tersely.

"Good night, Frank. Thank you very much for coming to my rescue."

Not even glancing her way, he gave a perfunctory nod of his head. She got out, and the car door was barely closed when he drove away and left her standing outside unit 5.

When she turned to go in, she realized that she didn't even have a key. She hated to wake up Mary Beth, but there didn't seem to be another choice. On her way to the office, she tried the knob of unit two on the chance that someone forgot to lock it.

Her guardian angel was watching over her. The knob turned in her hand. She went inside and found an exercise mat, spread it out on the floor and curled up on it, exhausted.

CARRIE WOKE EARLY and got an extra room key from Mary Beth—after she explained what had happened to her in Bowen.

"Good grief," Mary Beth said. "How awful. Is there anything I can do?"

"Let me eat on credit until I can get some cash?"

"Of course. Do you need any money?"

"I'll make arrangements with my uncle, but thanks for offering."

"Anything I can do, let me know."

Carrie went to her room, showered and spent the morning talking with Uncle Tuck, her bank and her credit card companies. She also checked with the sheriff's office in Bowen. Her car would be released that afternoon. Maybe she could ask Mary Beth to drive her over.

By eleven-thirty she was starving. Her food stash in the room was depleted, and she hadn't had a decent meal since—actually, she couldn't remember. She ran a brush through her hair and headed for the tearoom.

The smells coming from the place had her mouth watering before she opened the door. Not many people were there yet, and as she looked around, she was relieved that Frank wasn't there. She didn't see any of the Outlaws.

Florence seated her at a table for four, and Carrie waved to Mabel Fortney behind the cash register. When the waitress came with her raspberry tea, Carrie ordered potato and leek soup as well as pecan chicken with salad and herbed rice.

She ate every bite and was waiting for chocolate pie when J.J. came in the door. He smiled and nodded when she spotted him. He hung his hat on a rack by the door and walked to her table.

"Mind if I join you?"

"Not at all, if you don't mind consorting with a jailbird," she said.

He laughed and slid into a chair. "I consort with them all the time. I've been riding Sheriff Thurston high over that fiasco in Bowen. He didn't find out the details until this morning, and he's really embarrassed about what happened. The kid that arrested you is new, and he was scared to death. It was his first real crime of any consequence."

"He's a doofus."

"I'll give you that," J.J. said. "The sheriff said

you could pick up your car anytime after lunch. Want a ride over?''

"I'd love it if it isn't too much trouble."

"No trouble at all."

The waitress brought her pie and another glass of tea, then took J.J.'s order.

J.J. took a sip of tea. "Are you really a landman?"

"I am." Carrie explained the situation, and J.J. didn't seem nearly as bent out of shape about it as his brother had been. "When the dust settles a little, I'd like to talk to you and your family about leasing your land for possible oil exploration."

"If the terms are right, sounds good to me," he said.

Carrie had ordered another plate to go so that she'd have food for that night. The waitress brought it out with J.J.'s meal.

"If you'll excuse me," Carrie said, "I need to get back to my room and make another phone call. I need to get a replacement for my driver's license."

"I'll take care of that for you," J.J. said. "We can stop by the DPS office on the way to Bowen and pick up a temporary license."

"Thanks, J.J. You're a lifesaver."

"Glad to oblige."

As she was leaving the tearoom, Carrie met Frank coming in. She smiled and said hello to him.

"Hello, Carrie." He didn't smile or break stride.

His attitude hurt. But she didn't have anybody to blame but herself. Maybe with time they could patch things up. Then maybe letting their relationship cool would be best. After all, she wouldn't be around much longer.

"CARRIE JUST LEFT," J.J. said as Frank sat down.

"I know. I saw her. I'll be glad when she finishes her business and leaves Naconiche."

"Whoa, big brother. I thought you'd taken a shine to the lady."

"One of the things I can't abide is liars," Frank said, "and Carrie lied to all of us big-time." He would have said more, but he stopped to order.

"You know," J.J. said. "I've been thinking about that, and truthfully I can't come up with a single time that she actually lied. She might have skirted the truth a little, but she said she did research in other things besides genealogy. And she really is into genealogy. It's a hobby of hers, and—"

"Let's talk about something besides Carrie," Frank said sharply.

"Okay. You interested in leasing your part of the land for oil? Now that I'm about to have a family, I could sure use the extra money."

"That's talking about Carrie."

"No," J.J. said. "That's talking about a business decision. Your being all clabbered up at Carrie—about a little of nothing if you ask me—is another matter altogether."

"I don't recall asking you. Besides if the land she wants to lease includes the part that Clyde Burrows owns, it's a moot point anyhow."

"How so?"

"I don't remember the details, but we almost had a killing over the same thing some years ago, and Clyde was at the core of the mess. Things got very tense. Ask Pop about it."

"I'll do that."

Frank didn't comment further, but he planned to

ask his father about the incident, too. He might be soured on Carrie, but he didn't want her to get hurt. Everybody around here knew Clyde Burrows wasn't anybody to mess with. Crazy old coot.

"You and Carrie still gonna be in the Follies together?" J.J. asked.

Frank winced. He hadn't even thought of that. If he tried to back out, his mama would have his hide. Looked like he was going to have to talk to Carrie after all. They were scheduled to practice in unit two Thursday night. He wondered if she remembered.

CARRIE WAS SORRY that Frank was still in a snit. And men accused women of being petty! She wondered if he would even show up for their practice session the next night. She planned to be there.

A few minutes after one o'clock, J.J. knocked on her door. He took her by the DPS office for a temporary license, then drove her to the sheriff's office in Bowen.

Sheriff Thurston himself apologized to her for the snafu. A big-bellied man around sixty, the sheriff had a bulbous, blue-and-red veined nose and red hair going gray. He had the kind of ruddy complexion that showed years of sun damage, but he had the most startlingly beautiful shade of blue eyes she'd ever seen. His office was amazingly neat, and the walls were filled with plaques and photographs, testimony to many years on the job.

"I was out of town, and I just got back early this morning," he said. "We did get a couple of sets of prints off the passenger door of your car."

"One of them probably belongs to Judge Frank

Outlaw,'' Carrie said dryly. ''I think you can safely eliminate him as a subject.''

The sheriff cleared his throat. ''Uh, yes, ma'am.''

J.J. ducked his head to hide a grin.

''And we found your purse. I had Bobby out scouring those woods all morning.''

''Thank heavens!'' Carrie said.

The sheriff opened a large paper sack and handed her the black shoulder bag. She quickly sorted through the contents.

''Anything missing?''

''Cash, credit cards and my cell phone. At least my driver's license, my checkbook and my insurance papers are still here.''

''I'd like a list of everything that's missing,'' Sheriff Thurston said. ''And you might want to call the credit card company and your phone company to let them know about the theft.''

''I did that this morning,'' Carrie told him.

''Mind giving me the name of your phone company and your number? If the perp made a call before you canceled, that might help locate him. Same with the credit cards.''

Carrie did all the paperwork while J.J. and Sheriff Thurston chatted, then they all went downstairs to get her car. She was expecting to see nasty fingerprint powder everywhere, but it was freshly washed and gleaming clean.

The sheriff handed her the keys. ''If you don't mind, check it out to see that everything is there.''

She was relieved to find her briefcase in the trunk, the extra credit card she kept in the glove compartment for gas and Sonny and Cher still in the CD player.

"Everything is still here," Carrie told the sheriff.

After J.J. made sure she didn't need him anymore, he shoved off back to Naconiche.

"I'm right sorry for the bad things that happened to you in our town," the sheriff said, "but I'm glad I got the opportunity to meet such a nice lady." He smiled and stuck out his hand.

Sheriff Thurston was obviously a charmer and a veteran of politics. At least he hadn't called her "a pretty little lady." Carrie shook his hand and returned the smile. "Thank you. I might suggest that your deputy needs a little more experience before he's turned loose on the public again."

"Yes, ma'am. I've already given Bobby a dressing-down over his behavior, and I'll be watching him close. He's a good kid, just not seasoned yet. I hope you won't hold this against Bowen. We have a fine town here, and we want you to come back and see us every chance you get."

"I still have business in the area. I'll be back in a few days. In the meantime," Carrie said, "I see a branch of my cell phone company across the street. I think I'll go over and see about a replacement."

"Tell Paula Ann I said to give you her best deal."

"I'll do that, Sheriff Thurston. Thank you."

He touched the brim of his hat. "Afternoon, ma'am."

In no time, Carrie had a new phone number, a complimentary phone and a cash advance from the credit card in the glove compartment. On her way back to Naconiche, she called Uncle Tuck and gave him her new number. He sounded worried, but she assured him that she was fine.

"First thing tomorrow morning, I'm going to begin

leasing property," she told him. "I'm going to start with a man named Clyde Burrows. I understand that he's the toughest sale. I figure he just needs a little sweet-talkin'."

Uncle Tuck laughed. "If anybody can sweet-talk him, darlin', you can."

Carrie hung up, turned up the volume of the CD player and sang with Sonny and Cher as she drove back to the Twilight Inn.

## Chapter Fourteen

Armed with a box of warm doughnuts and cookies from the bakery, Carrie set out bright and early for Clyde Burrows's house. He was supposed to be an ornery old cuss, but she'd learned early on that old saying was true about the way to a man's heart being through his stomach. She was simply going calling with her goodies and "set a spell."

She didn't get any farther than the gate. It was chained and padlocked. A couple of toots on the horn didn't raise a soul; the noise only set a pack of hounds barking and braying.

She honked again—louder.

The hounds grew louder.

Not discouraged, Carrie filled the pockets of her jeans with doggie treats, hooked her pepper spray on her belt and looped the strap of her bag over her head and one arm. She balanced the bakery box on a post and started climbing over the rail fence. When she was about to throw one leg over the top, the hounds of hell came thundering from a stand of trees on a rise. Barking and braying, the wild-eyed pack of half a dozen or more rawboned animals gathered at the fence. She felt like a treed raccoon.

"Hello, boys and girls," she cooed. "Just calm down. I'm a friend. See?" She tossed a handful of doggie treats down to them and waited.

They scarfed up the treats and, tails wagging, looked up for more. These were hunting dogs, not guard dogs, and they seemed more loud and ill-mannered than vicious. She tossed them another handful of tidbits and considered climbing on over.

She might be brave, but she wasn't insane.

A shotgun blast peppered the bushes a few feet to her left, and she froze.

"Leave them dogs alone," a gravelly voice yelled. "You're ruinin' them. And get out of here." He whistled and the dogs went loping off.

"Mr. Burrows?" she yelled back.

"Who wants to know?"

"I'm Carrie Campbell, and I want to talk to you."

"'Bout what?"

"Can we talk without yelling?" She started to throw her other leg over. Another blast a few feet to her right stopped her cold. "Is that any way to greet a visitor? I just want to have a few words with you, and I've brought doughnuts."

"What kind?"

"Plain glazed and strawberry-filled. And I have macaroons and brownies, too."

A grizzled old man in overalls and a dirty cap emerged from the woods. He sported stringy hair, an unkempt beard and a twelve-gauge shotgun. One eye was squinted, but when the other one had a chance to look her over, he let out a cackle of laughter. "Be damned if it ain't the singin' gal."

Carrie studied him closely, too. This was the old geezer in the rusty pickup that she'd met at stoplights a couple of times. She grinned. "That's me. I was practicing."

"Practicing what?"

"I'm going to be in the Naconiche Fall Follies, and I've been rehearsing the words to the songs. I sometimes get a little carried away."

"You ain't here to sell me tickets, are you?"

She laughed. "Nope. I want to talk to you about something else. May I come in?"

"Come on up to the porch. And bring them sweets." He turned and walked away without waiting for her.

Carrie climbed down, retrieved the bakery box and hurried after him.

Over the rise was an unpainted ramshackle house with five or six steps leading up to a long porch. The hounds had taken their place under the front of the house and a couple of chickens pecked at the bare dirt around the place. The roof was weathered tin and a wide, open hallway, called a dog run, split the house down the middle.

Three straight chairs, crudely fashioned of unpainted wood, sat on the porch. Their seats were cowhide with the hair left on—though some spots were worn bare of bristles. The chairs might have been ten years old or a hundred. Clyde Burrows was nowhere around.

Carrie didn't go looking. She waited on the porch.

Clyde soon appeared with two stained mugs. "Brought coffee. Sit down."

She sat down in one of the chairs and put the sweets on the chair next to her. He handed her a mug and took the other chair. The coffee was tar black, scalding hot and tasted like burned peanut shells.

"Boy, that's coffee," she said, opening the bakery box. "What's your favorite?"

"I believe you picked every one of them," he said, looking over the assortment. "I'm right partial to coconut." He selected a macaroon and reared back, leaning against the wall with the chair resting on its back two legs.

Carrie took a plain doughnut and ate it slowly while he devoured a brownie and half a jelly doughnut. "Pretty place you got here."

"I like it."

"Run any cattle?"

"'Bout twenty head." He licked his fingers.

"Hogs?"

"Fatting two for meat and lard."

"I love cracklin's."

"Come around during the first good cold snap, and I'll be boilin' some down."

"You got a deal," Carrie said. She waited for him to pick up the next thread of conversation.

"You like singin'?"

"Sure do. I'm in the car a lot, and I often sing along with the radio or a CD."

"Me, too. Don't have a CD player, and my radio's busted. Folks see me singin' to myself and say I've got a screw loose."

"What do they know? What kind of songs do you sing?"

"Mostly country. Amuse myself in the evening pickin' and singin'."

"Oh?" Carrie said. "What instrument?"

"Guitar mostly. Some banjo. What kind of song you singin' in the show?" he asked, clearly through with self-disclosure.

"Two kinds. One is 'Diamonds Are a Girl's Best Friend' from an old movie with Marilyn Monroe."

"Seen it when I was in the army. Korea. She's dead, you know."

"I heard."

"Think she killed herself?" He selected another macaroon.

"I don't know. Hard to imagine. My friend Kelly Martin and I are doing the song in the Fall Follies."

"The doctor lady?"

Carrie nodded. "And Frank Outlaw and I are singing another song. One of Sonny and Cher's hits. I'm Cher."

"Figured." Clyde cackled. "Be hard to picture the judge with hair down to his waist and his navel showing."

She grinned at the idea. "Yeah, it would. You ever see Sonny and Cher?"

He nodded. "On the TV. Right 'fore I went to Nam."

"You were in Vietnam, too?"

"Yep. Stayed in after Korea. Made sergeant. Went to Nam and got shot all to sh—'scuse me—pieces. Lost my eye."

"I'm so sorry, Mr. Burrows."

"Everybody just calls me Clyde. Sometimes they call me 'that crazy old coot.'" He gave another cackle.

"I think, like my uncle always says, that you're crazy like a fox."

"There's that. You ready to state your business?"

"If you'll promise not to shoot me."

A little bit of a smile flashed at one corner of his

mouth, and he covered it by brushing crumbs from his beard. "I ain't one to promise."

"Then I guess I'll have to take my chances." She broke off part of a brownie and ate it to fortify herself. "Fact is, I'm a landman for my uncle's oil company."

"I don't hold with oil companies raping the land," he said sharply.

"Neither do I. Now just wait and hear me out. Oil companies don't do things the way they used to, throwing up a derrick every few feet and making a mess. Nowadays, they're more concerned with the environment. If you would lease your land to us, any well we drill might not even be on your property. It might be on your neighbor's. We group landowners into units, and if oil or gas is found, everybody in the unit shares the proceeds. And we can write certain things into the contract, like not putting a well within a certain distance to, say, ponds or streams or your house or your pigpen for that matter."

He frowned as if he were mulling over her remarks.

"And you have to remember, we might even come up dry. I'm offering a hundred dollars an acre for a five-year lease on the mineral rights. That's more than enough to buy a fancy new pickup."

His eyebrows went up. "I been thinking about a new pickup. One I got now's held together with rust and baling wire. Passed by the dealer's lot a couple of times. Had my eye on a green one, but those new ones are higher than a cat's back."

"You could afford that pickup—with a radio and a CD player—and a new tractor, too."

"Tractor runs fine. But my middlebuster's broke."

They dickered a few more minutes, and Carrie

brought out the contract in her bag. She went over it word by word, and after a few changes, Clyde Burrows signed on the dotted line.

Carrie explained how payment would be made and gave him her card with her new cell phone number written on it. "You can reach me anytime at that number on the back."

"Ain't got a telephone," Clyde said.

"I'll be staying at the Twilight Inn for a while if you have any questions."

He nodded. "Come back again. Nice settin' with a pretty lady. And I got a kick out of watching you sing in your car. You're spirited for sure. Most folks light a shuck when I unload a round of buckshot in their vicinity."

She grinned. "I considered it." She stood and stuck out her hand. "I'll want a ride in that new pickup."

"Deal." He stood and shook her hand. "I'll go open the gate for you."

As they walked from his house he said, "You like country music?"

"Sure do."

"Come around if you're out this way some evenin', and we'll do some singin'."

Carrie grinned at the thought. "You're on."

ONCE CARRIE was in her car and out of earshot, she laughed and let out a rebel yell. Hot damn, she was on a roll. Talk about lucky—her guardian angel must have been pulling a few strings when she'd drawn up by Clyde Burrows at those stoplights. He'd gotten a kick out of catching her singing in her car. Probably figured they were kindred spirits. Truth was, she kind of liked the old coot. And he didn't seem particularly mean or crazy to her. Odd maybe, but shoot, she thought odd folks were interesting.

Deciding that she might as well stop by to see Clyde's nephew while she was in the neighborhood, she located his house down the road.

She found Vernon Burrows working on a tractor that looked older than he was. A tall, slender man in patched jeans and a chambray shirt, he was clean-shaven and soft-spoken. He was a farmer who supplemented his income by driving a school bus, and from the looks of his place, some extra cash would be a godsend to his large family. When she stated her business, you would have thought she'd offered him the keys to the mint, then his face fell.

"You're not likely to lease any property around here unless you get my uncle to agree to it first. And he's a hard man to deal with."

After she told him that Clyde had agreed, Vernon was incredulous at first. When she convinced him that his uncle had signed a lease agreement, he was eager to sign, as well.

So far, so good.

Wes Outlaw was next on her list. Maybe she could catch him at the Double Dip. She called on her cell phone to make sure he was around.

"He isn't here right now," Miss Nonie said, "but I except him back any minute. Anything I can help you with?"

"No, thank you. I'll stop by when I get back to town."

When Carrie walked into the shop a few minutes later, Wes wasn't there, but Frank was. He sat at the counter, having a cup of coffee and talking with his mother.

"Hi, Miss Nonie. Hi, Frank."

Frank merely nodded, but his mother said, "Hello, Carrie. Wes isn't back yet, but he shouldn't be long."

"I'll wait." Carrie glanced at her watch. "I don't think an ice-cream cone would ruin my lunch, do you, Miss Nonie? I'll have my usual, please—a single today."

"Coming right up," Nonie said.

Carrie sat down two stools away from Frank, studying him while he sipped his coffee. He seemed to be pointedly ignoring her. No skin off her nose if he wanted to sulk.

"Here you go. One dip of peppermint with chocolate sprinkles."

Carrie took the ice-cream cone and handed Miss Nonie the money for it. As was her custom, she closed her eyes and savored the smell before her tongue swiped the side of the scoop. She took another lick and gave a little moan of pleasure before she glanced up.

Frank was staring at her, his cup resting at his lips.

A little devil made her take a very long lick of the ice cream. Her eyes locked with his; she sighed deeply and moaned softly again. "What can I say?" She smiled at Frank. "It's an orgasmic experience."

His nostrils flared briefly, and he looked away.

Miss Nonie tittered.

"Well, Mama, if you'll excuse me, I have to get back to the office." Frank's cup clattered into the saucer, and he started out the door at a fast clip.

"Don't forget tonight!" Carrie called after him.

He stopped. "Tonight?"

"Practice. For the Sonny and Cher number. Seven o'clock in unit two at the Inn."

Frank glanced between Carrie and his mother. "Seven. Right." And then he was out the door.

Miss Nonie cleared her throat. "You two have a falling-out?"

"He did. I didn't." She started to tell Miss Nonie about the reason for Frank's irritation with her.

"No need to explain unless you just want a sounding board," the older woman said. "I've already heard about it. Everybody in town is talking, and, given the way news travels around here, makes perfect sense to me that you didn't come in and announce your business right away. Frank's a reasonable man. He'll get over his pique soon enough."

The bell over the door tinkled, and Wes Outlaw came in. He greeted Carrie and leaned over the counter to kiss Miss Nonie.

Wes took a stool next to Carrie. "Glad to see you got your car back. Sorry about that mess over in Bowen. I carried Sheriff Thurston high about the dangerous desperado his deputy captured, but Red's a good man. I've known him for years."

"He seemed nice," Carrie said. "And very embarrassed."

"They already found the kid who robbed you and the store. He's cooling his heels in a jail just over the state line in Louisiana. No sign of your stuff on him, Red said."

"Figures. I need to talk to you for a few minutes if this is a good time."

"Good as any," Wes said. "Let's go sit at that table over in the corner in case somebody comes in.

And take your time finishing that cone. Peppermint is my favorite, too.''

"I'm almost done.'' She took another couple of bites and threw the rest of the cone into the trash on the way to the corner table. Wiping her fingers on a napkin, she was about to broach the subject of leasing when Wes stopped her.

"I might can save you some trouble,'' he said. "If this is about leasing mineral rights around here…''

"It is.''

"You're wasting your time, Carrie. I could have told you that right off.''

"You won't lease your part of the rights on the Outlaw land? I heard you stymied an oil deal several years ago.''

"I'm not your problem. Didn't really stymie the deal back then, either. We've got some mighty peculiar folks in these parts, and you're not likely to get past them. Last time this came up, things got hot and we almost had a couple of killings. I might not be sheriff anymore, but I don't like to see anybody go asking for trouble, either. I've become right fond of you, Carrie, and I'd hate like rip for you to get hurt.''

Carrie smiled. "I'm tougher than I look. Tougher than a two-dollar steak, my uncle says. In my business I've learned to deal with all kinds, and I can hold my own with just about anybody—even the ornery cusses. Is Clyde Burrows the one you're warning me about?''

Wes nodded. "The man's dangerous. I could tell you some stories…well, that's neither here nor there. If Clyde owns any of the land you want to lease, you can forget the deal. He won't have any part of it.''

"If Clyde agrees to lease to me, will you? And will

you encourage others as well? Hundred dollars an acre.''

Wes shook his head. ''I don't want you going near Clyde's place. It's not safe.''

She grinned. ''Too late. I've already been. And I've got his name on the dotted line.''

''Clyde? *Clyde* Burrows?''

''Yep.''

Wes sat back in his chair. ''I gotta hear this.''

# Chapter Fifteen

By the time Carrie and Wes Outlaw had finished their business, it was nearing the lunch hour, and Carrie wasn't at all hungry. An idea came to her.

"Miss Nonie," she said, "seems to me that you're always stuck here and never get to go out to lunch. How about I tend the shop while you and Wes go to the tearoom?"

Acting flustered, Nonie said, "Oh, Carrie, I couldn't ask you to do that."

"You're not asking. I'm offering. Wes, wouldn't you like a lunch date with your wife?"

"I surely would," he said with a wink.

Carrie went behind the counter. "Show me where everything is and how to work the cash register, then go. I can handle it."

"Are you sure?"

"Positive. Give me your apron."

Nonie relinquished her white bibbed apron, then instructed Carrie in the basics. Nonie had a spring in her step as she pulled off her hair net and gave her curls a pat on the way out the door with Wes.

Carrie couldn't help but grin. They were such darlings.

The hair net reminded her that she needed to do something about her own hair in case the health inspector made a surprise visit. She found a rubber band in her purse and a red ball cap hanging on a peg in the back room. She quickly gathered her hair into a ponytail, pulled on the cap and scrubbed her hands.

She was just drying off when the bell over the front door tinkled. It was Millie the librarian.

Millie looked startled. "Where's Miss Nonie?"

"Out on a lunch date. I'm filling in. What will you have?"

"A large hot fudge sundae with pecans."

"Whipped cream?" Carrie asked as she scooped out the vanilla.

"Yes. Lots of it. I always allow myself one decadent treat a week in place of lunch."

Carrie grinned. "Beats the heck out of a ham sandwich." She ladled hot fudge over the ice cream, sprinkled on pecans and topped her creation with a generous squirt of canned whipped cream. She set the sundae on the counter in front of Millie. "How's that?"

"Lovely."

They chatted a few minutes while Carrie made change, then Carrie said, "I'd like to make an appointment to see you sometime this week."

"Is it about leasing our property?"

"Does everybody already know?"

Millie laughed. "Just about. My brother and I would love to lease to you, but I'm afraid there are one or two others in the area who will make it impossible."

"If you're talking about Clyde Burrows, he has already signed a contract."

Millie's eyes widened. "You're kidding."

"Nope."

A merchant from down the street came in for two cups of strawberry to go, so Carrie left Millie to her sundae.

There was a steady trickle of customers, enough to keep Carrie busy but nothing she couldn't handle. She was managing fine, she thought—until she saw the chartered bus stop outside.

In two minutes she was deluged with senior citizens wanting ice cream, gift items and directions to the bathroom. She pasted on a smile and gave it her best shot. It was chaos.

"Where's Mama?" a gruff voice said beside her.

She glanced up. Frank. Scowling. "Out to lunch. Would you hand me that banana? And take off your coat. I need some help here."

He took off his coat, rolled up his sleeves and went to work. They made a pretty good team.

By the time the last senior citizen had boarded the bus a half hour later, they were laughing and having a great time.

Carrie leaned against the ice-cream case and blew out a big *whew*. "I feel like I've just survived a stampede. Does that happen often?"

"Once or twice a week. When I saw the bus, I came over to lend a hand. Whoever in the family is available usually pitches in to help."

"Thanks. I couldn't have made it without you."

"You were doing very well."

"Thanks. I was going crazy. Anyhow, we made a tidy sum for your mom. I'm going to reward myself with another peppermint cone. Want one?"

He smiled. "I don't think so."

"Aw, come on. Live dangerously. I'll dip. What's your favorite flavor?"

"Praline."

"Good choice." She piled two scoops on a cone and handed it to him with a little bow. "There you go. Are you over your snit?"

"My *snit?* Judges don't have snits."

"Oh? What do they have?" She dug out two scoops of peppermint and liberally covered the top with chocolate sprinkles.

"Judges take things under serious advisement."

"And?"

"And J.J. says I overreacted. My mother says I overreacted. My dad says I'm as stubborn as a splinter. They're probably right, but it still smarts a little."

"I'm truly sorry that I had to mislead anybody, but when I first arrived, I really didn't know who to trust with the truth. Then later, well, I couldn't seem to find the right moment to explain to you."

They ate their cones in silence for a moment.

"I understand," he said.

"Do you?"

Frank nodded. "But you've got a major problem. Clyde Burrows. He won't let anybody connected with an oil company set foot on his property. I don't want you trying to go out to his place and get shot. He's a terror with that twelve-gauge he totes. Promise me that you won't go charging out there alone. Let J.J. and Dad and me—"

"Too late."

"What's too late?"

"I went to see Clyde first thing this morning."

"And he didn't try to shoot you?"

"Naw. Both barrels were at least ten feet shy."

"My God!" Frank tossed aside his cone and grabbed her upper arms. "That bastard! I'll—"

"Just cool it, Your Honor. He didn't hurt me. As a matter of fact, we're big buddies now. We're kindred spirits."

"You and *Clyde Burrows?*"

"Yep." She related the story of their meeting.

Frank could only shake his head. "I never would have believed it. Have you talked to Dad about leasing yet? He still owns half the mineral rights to the whole Outlaw property."

"I know. I talked to him before he took your mom to lunch. He's agreeable."

"Then I won't stand in your way."

"Thanks, Frank. Truthfully, I didn't know until a few days ago that your property would be involved."

"I believe you. Now I have to get back to court."

The quick kiss he started to give her turned into a longer one. His lips were cool and tasted of pralines.

It might have gone on forever, but the jingle of the bell made them jerk apart. Nonie and Wes stood there smiling.

"Looks like you two have made up," Wes said.

Frank just grinned and grabbed his coat. "I'm late."

After he was gone, Nonie nodded to the pink streams trickling down Carrie's hand. "Your ice cream is melting."

Her ice cream wasn't the only thing melting. Her heart was a mere puddle.

THAT EVENING, unit two at the Twilight Inn was a madhouse. Somebody had gotten the schedule screwed up and four acts had shown up to practice, including the Beatles, ten flappers from the roaring twenties and Elvis.

"Tell you what," Carrie said to Patsy, their assistant director. "Since there are just the two of us, Frank and I can go practice in my room."

"And we can practice in the tearoom," Mary Beth said. She, along with Dixie, Ellen and seven others, were flappers.

"I'll just hang out here," Elvis said. "I haven't got anything better to do."

Carrie grinned all the way to her room. She finally had a good excuse to be alone with Frank, and nobody in the town could gossip about such an innocent activity.

Once she unlocked the door, she stepped aside for Frank to enter. Only the lamp on the desk was on to cast a dim glow over the room; she didn't switch on other lights. The moment she closed the door, Carrie turned the dead bolt, slid the security chain in place and said, "Now I've got you, babe."

Frank chuckled as he took her into his arms. "You've had me for a long time, babe. Do you even have a tape player in the room?"

"Of course I do. We can actually practice. Later." She slipped her arms around his neck and pulled him down as she reached for his mouth with hers.

He didn't need any coaxing. His lips were hungry, demanding, and as his tongue invaded deeply, she went hot all over.

She wanted to rip off her clothes and drag him to bed, but when she reached for the buttons on her blouse, Frank pushed her hands away.

"Here. Let me. I want to savor this for a while."

He undid the buttons on her blouse slowly, kissing

her face softly as each was freed. Her eyes, her cheeks, her nose. He nuzzled her throat as he slowly pulled the tails free from her waistband, moved to her chest as he tossed the blouse aside.

His tongue made a slow journey along the top curves of her breasts as he unhooked her bra.

She was dying.

When her bra fell away, his lips and tongue moved slowly over her breasts. "I've dreamed of this," he whispered.

The tip of his tongue teased her nipple, and with a little cry, she pressed herself closer to his mouth.

It was sweet agony.

Fumbling for the buttons of his shirt, she said, "I want to feel your skin against mine."

His shirt joined hers, and the kisses and caresses grew more feverish as the rest of their clothes were shed and they stood skin against skin.

Frank groaned as he lifted her against him. He was hard and ready, begging entry as her legs went around his waist. She was doing her best to oblige.

"Wait! Wait!" he said. "Protection. Where are my pants?"

"Who knows?" She kissed him deeply, her heart pounding, her breath ragged. "Look in the night-stand."

He carried her to the bed and sat down with her. She fumbled in the drawer for the box, then ripped it open. Little packets went flying everywhere, but she managed to snag one. "Here." She thrust it at him.

He seemed to have ten thumbs, and just as he got the packet open, he dropped it. "Damn!"

Carrie grabbed another one. "I'll do it. Lie down."

Her hands weren't much steadier, but between the

two of them, they managed to get the deed done. She straddled his hips and began to slowly lower herself onto him.

When she started to move, his hands held her still. "Don't move for a minute or I'm gone." He rolled over with her so that he was in control.

He kissed her gently, then fire flashed and they were both gone. Things were hard and fast, and her climax broke just as he stiffened and shuddered.

After a moment, he kissed her nose. "Sorry about that. It's been a long time for me."

"Don't apologize. It's been a while for me, too."

He rolled over and drew her close, and they simply snuggled for several minutes, basking in their new closeness, lost in their own thoughts.

"I'm hungry," Carrie said.

Frank chuckled. "Me, too. You have anything in that tiny refrigerator of yours?"

"I'll check."

She got up and went into the bathroom and pulled on a nightshirt. She wasn't quite comfortable enough to run around nude in front of him. After studying her stash, she filled a paper plate with a few odds and ends from the kitchenette corner.

Carrie slipped her new CD into the portable player and returned to bed, and noticed that Frank was wearing underwear. Burgundy. Very sexy.

"I'm sorry you dressed," he said. "I was looking forward to enjoying the view."

She looked pointedly at his shorts. "Me, too."

He stirred. She chuckled. It promised to be a delightful rehearsal.

They sang along with Sonny and Cher while they fed each other grapes and peanut butter crackers.

DRIVING HOME that night Frank told himself that he should feel guilty, but he refused to consider it. He felt too damned good to feel guilty. Sated. Mellow. Good. Better than good. The first time had been good, the second extraordinary.

His "snit" hadn't lasted long. He grinned when he thought about Carrie's term. She wasn't much of one to waltz around anything. And he couldn't believe that she'd faced Clyde Burrows and his gun head-on—and won him over. She was gutsy for sure. He liked that about her. He liked a lot about her. They were well matched.

Truth was, he understood the reason for her discretion about her job. She hadn't blatantly lied for any illegal or immoral purpose. And it wasn't as if they had any sort of committed relationship. They were simply...what? Friends? Lovers? They hadn't even been that early on. What were they now? He didn't try to examine the situation too much. He just planned to enjoy himself while it lasted.

He hummed a bar, then started singing "I Got You Babe" in his best Sonny Bono imitation.

CARRIE WAS busy the next day making appointments and visiting with property owners out in the county. Late getting to the tearoom for lunch, she barely made it before closing. Frank had already eaten and gone, J.J. told her. He dragged up a chair and kept her company while she ate.

"Glad to hear you two aren't on the outs anymore," J.J. said. "He was acting as goofy as a wall-eyed frog."

Carrie chuckled but declined to comment further. She didn't tell J.J. how very well things were going between Frank and her. He was a wonderful lover—virile, thoughtful and thorough. The best.

She was sorry to have missed Frank at lunch, but they'd made a date to go riding later that afternoon. When it started raining about two-thirty, she was heartsick, thinking that they wouldn't be able to ride, but the skies cleared after a quick downpour. A norther had blown through and the air turned a bit nippy. Being used to the foibles of Texas weather, she had packed a few warm clothes as well as shorts. A red cotton turtleneck felt good under her jean jacket.

Frank had the horses saddled when she arrived, and the twins were nowhere in sight. She didn't ask about them.

Carrie stroked Betsy and talked to her before mounting, while Betsy was on her best behavior. "Riding Betsy brings back a lot of good memories."

"Of Calico?"

"Yes. I didn't realize how much I missed riding—or her."

"Did I remember to tell you that I checked Betsy's papers? By an amazing coincidence Betsy and Calico *are* related. It's good to know that a part of your horse lives on in her great-granddaughter."

"I'm not sure I believe in coincidences, either," Carrie said, patting Betsy's neck. "Sometimes I think things are part of a grand design."

"I can't argue with that."

They rode the property for almost an hour before heading back to the corral. After the horses were tended, they went inside to watch the taped special showing clips of Sonny and Cher.

"You know," Carrie said. "I think we might just be better than they are."

They ran through their number twice, adding gestures they'd noted on the tape. They were about to sing it again when the twins burst into the house announcing that they were starving. Seems that they'd been to the grocery store with the housekeeper.

"Hold your horses, kids," Matilda said. "That pot roast I put on ought to be just about done."

"Is that what I've been smelling?" Frank asked. "I hope you'll stay and have dinner with us," he said to Carrie. "Matilda makes the best pot roast in East Texas."

"I wouldn't want to impose."

"Please stay," Janey said. "Please, please, please? I want to show you my princess costume."

"Halloween is this weekend," Frank said.

"I'm going to be Spiderman," Jimmy said.

"I'd forgotten about Halloween," Carrie said.

"It's obvious you don't have kids. We always go trick-or-treating and then have a party. We have a big weekend planned. Think you can brave a couple of dozen kids?"

*Not on my best day,* Carrie thought.

"Oh, please come," Janey said. "It will be so much fun. We bob for apples and everything."

"Oh, darn," Carrie said. "I wish I could, but I have to go to Houston this weekend."

"You're not leaving for good, are you?" Frank said.

"Oh, no. I still have lots of work to do around here for a while yet. I just need to tend to some things. I'm sure to have a huge pile of mail that I should sort through. If you'd like, I can check into some Sonny and Cher costumes while I'm there.''

''What kind of costumes? I'd just figured on wearing jeans and an old vest with some fringe or something on it. As a matter of fact, I think I have an old fleece-lined jacket that I could cut the sleeves out of, and use the lining for a vest. Reminds me of one that Sonny wore. This is just for one performance.''

She would have begged off dinner, but the smells coming from the kitchen and the coaxing from Frank and the family finally won her over.

The pot roast was superb. The kids were reasonably well mannered, and the housekeeper, who lived in and took care of the kids, was a hoot.

After dessert and after seeing the twins' Halloween costumes, Frank walked her to her car.

Smiling, he said, ''Wish I could invite you for a sleepover.''

''Something tells me that wouldn't be wise.''

''Smart lady.''

He gave her a brief kiss. ''I can hardly wait to *practice* again in your room.''

She grinned. ''We'll turn the music up very loud to drown out the other noise.''

He kissed her again. ''Good idea. I like the way you squeal, but others may get the wrong idea.''

Carrie reached up for one last kiss, but a cry of ''Daddy!'' jerked them apart.

''Sorry,'' Frank said. ''Duty calls.''

# Chapter Sixteen

By noon on Saturday, Carrie was on her way to Houston, singing along with the latest Celine Dion CD. She'd gotten up early and packed the things she'd be needing, detoured by Bowen to talk to the two landowners there and secured their lease agreements.

She was eager to get back to the city, inhale a little pollution and rev up her metabolism. While she was in town, she planned to have lunch at her favorite Greek place in the Village, do some serious shopping at the Galleria and do a little partying with a more sophisticated crowd.

Diane Turner would know where the parties were. Carrie dialed the real estate agency where Diane worked and luckily found her in.

"How in the world are you, Carrie? I haven't heard from you in ages. Are you in town?"

"I'm on my way there and desperately in need of something fun to do this weekend. What's going on?"

As she expected, Diane knew all the events and details. Carrie begged off a costume party that evening, but they made plans to go to a big blowout in Piney Point on Sunday night.

When Carrie arrived at her town house, she found a musty smell and a huge pile of mail in the front hall. After she opened a few windows, she tackled the mail. Most of it was junk, which she pitched; most of the rest were bills, which she paid. She tossed a load of laundry into the washer, made several phone calls, then found she had the rest of the afternoon and evening with nothing to do. Her biweekly service kept her place clean. Since she was gone so much, her only indoor plants were silk and the outdoor ones were maintained by a regular crew, so she couldn't groom her potted fern or putter in the dirt.

Perhaps she should have taken up Diane on the costume party.

Costume. An idea struck her. Maybe she could find something Cher-ish at one of the vintage shops nearby. She grabbed her keys and took off.

At the second store she visited, Carrie hit it lucky. She found low-riding bell-bottoms that fit perfectly and a peasant blouse with long billowy sleeves that she bought for a little of nothing. She also found a poet shirt that she thought would fit Frank, and re-minded her of one she'd seen Sonny wear on the special they'd watched.

After stashing her purchases in the car, she bought a soft pretzel at the little bakery next door and started down the street to a pottery shop that she loved. On the way she spotted a small wig store with a going-out-of-business banner across the front window. Wouldn't it be a kick if she found a cheap Cher-style wig?

It was probably a long shot, but she finished her pretzel, licked her fingers and went in.

When Carrie told the tiny woman wearing a sari

what she was looking for, the proprietor said, "I got just the thing."

She dug through a bargain barrel of hair that was marked $5.00 and came up with a long mop of shiny black stuff that wouldn't have fooled anybody up close. Yet when Carrie tried it on she saw that, with a little trimming and styling, it was perfect for the stage. Better yet, she found a medium-length brown one for Frank. Giggling at the thought of Frank in that wig, she bought them both.

After spending half an hour in the pottery shop, she decided on a beautifully thrown fruit bowl as a wedding gift for Mary Beth and J.J., a bud vase that would look perfect in Kelly's kitchen and a small raku pot for herself because she fell in love with it.

She stopped by a specialty market and bought scrumptious-looking shrimp salad, asparagus vinaigrette and a small baguette for her dinner, and wonderful huge bagels and cream cheese for the next morning.

Problem was, later she only picked at her food as she sat in front of the TV in her living room. Despite the noise on Channel 2, the place seemed oppressively quiet and sterile. There was no life around her—nothing to keep her company. No dog, no cat, no canary. She didn't even have an ivy or a sweet potato vine in the kitchen window. She was the only living, breathing creature in the entire house. The walls seemed to close in on her. To escape the claustrophobia, she went to the nearest mall, bought a ton of things she didn't need and went to a movie she'd been wanting to see. The movie was boring, and she left in the middle.

Carrie went home and polished her toenails.

Exciting night in the city.

Wonder what Frank was doing. Did he miss her?

SUNDAY WASN'T much better. There was some sort of goofy temperature inversion, and a blanket of haze hung over the city reeking of exhaust fumes and chemical plant wastes. Hoping that most of it would burn off by noon, Carrie spent the morning straightening her closet.

She called two or three acquaintances looking for a lunch partner, but nobody was available. Even Uncle Tuck and Sam were out of town. She went to the Greek restaurant alone.

It was crowded, and she had to wait forty-five minutes for a tiny table by the kitchen. The food was good, but it would have been better if she'd had someone to share it with.

The only things she bought at Neimans were some hand lotion and a trendy outfit for the party that night. She wandered around the Galleria for a few minutes, but only a pretty little fish in a decorative vase caught her eye. A live plant protruded from the vase's neck, and the black and red fish swam among the roots. Carrie bought it, took it home and put it on the coffee table.

The party turned out to be a bust. At least it was for her. Diane and the others crammed into the huge house on Houston's affluent west side seemed to be having a sensational time. It was crowded, loud and frenetic. Food and liquor flowed freely, and she was hit on at least three times by guys who were high on Lord knows what. All of them were rich, well-tanned and well-toned. None of them was the least bit appealing.

There were people in town who would have given a month's salary for an invitation to the bash where she was. All she got out of the party was a headache.

When the wife of one of the town's young movers and shakers started moving and shaking on top of the pool table in her bra and thong, Carrie only rolled her eyes. Going trick-or-treating or to a football game in Naconiche would have been more fun than this.

She found Diane in a lip-lock with the young mover and shaker—or someone remarkably like him—said her goodbyes and called a taxi.

The next morning she packed, strapped her fish into the passenger seat and went back to Naconiche.

Was she nuts? she asked herself as she drove. Who in their right mind would prefer Naconiche to Houston?

"Things are getting out of hand when you begin to prefer a motel room in a hick town to a great town house in Houston," Carrie said to the fish. Then she sighed. "I can't believe I'm talking to a fish."

"CAN YOU BELIEVE I was actually talking to a fish?" Carrie said to Kelly as they sipped tea in Kelly's den. They'd spent most of Kelly's Monday lunch hour practicing. "Can you believe I actually *bought* a fish? With a *plant* on top for goshsakes."

"The human need for companionship," Kelly said. "Remember that movie with Tom Hanks? The one where he was stranded alone on an island?"

"Yeah. His best friend was a soccer ball."

"What did you name him?" Kelly asked.

"Who?"

"The fish."

"I haven't named it. And I don't know if it's a him or a her. How about Monroe in honor of our song?"

"Works for me. Want to run through the number again?"

Carrie shook her head. "I think we've done enough for today. We've got it down pat. We can have another run-through Thursday night after aerobics class. My biggest concern is that we might scandalize the town with those costumes." She pointed to the skimpy black satin outfits draped over the back of the couch.

"Maybe with the black fishnet stockings they won't look so…"

"Sinful?"

Kelly chuckled. "I was thinking more along the lines of revealing."

"Dream on. If they were cut any higher we would have to staple them on."

"Does it bother you?"

"Not me," Carrie said. "I don't have to live here. I'll be gone a few days after the show."

"I wish you weren't leaving," Kelly said. "It's been nice having a special girlfriend."

"Spending time with you and getting reacquainted has been terrific," Carrie said, "and I don't want for us to lose touch again, but my work will soon take me to heaven knows where. And there's really nothing for me here."

"What about Frank Outlaw?"

"What about him?"

"I thought things might be getting a little serious between you two."

Carrie shook her head. "He's a great guy and I'm very fond of him, but he has two kids and a dead wife who are the center of his life. And rightly so. One of these days, when he's ready, he'll find the perfect woman and marry her. I'm not her.''

''Why not?''

''We've discussed this before. I'm not the marrying, mothering kind. And there's my job.'' Squirming at the direction of their conversation, Carrie jumped up. ''I almost forgot. I brought you a present. It's in the car. Be right back.''

FRANK HAD PASSED the Twilight Inn a dozen times or more since Saturday. His eyes always went to the door of number five. He'd gotten so used to having lunch with Carrie that Monday without her had been strange, and he'd picked up the phone several times to call her, then remembered that she was probably still in Houston. He couldn't believe how much he'd missed her.

Too much.

He'd better get used to it. Before long she would be finished with her work here and be gone for good. He was torn between the need to start weaning himself away from her and the urge to get in all the time with her that he could. When he spotted her car in its slot late Monday afternoon, the latter won. His car turned into the motel lot like one of Pavlov's dogs.

When she opened the door to his knock, Frank didn't think he'd ever seen such a beautiful sight. She had on a short terry robe, and a towel was wrapped around her hair. Her skin glowed. And her smile knocked him on his butt.

''Well, hello,'' she said in a sultry voice.

''Hello, yourself. Looks like I interrupted something.''

"Nothing exciting. Come on in before the local folks get an eyeful of me undressed."

"You're dressed," he said, his gaze zeroing in on the deep cleavage revealed by her robe's gap. His imagination had X-ray vision and was going wild.

"Just barely." She chuckled and stepped back to allow him into the room.

He didn't need to be coaxed. He was in the door, and she was in his arms quicker than he could bang a gavel.

God, she tasted good. And smelled good. And felt good. He tossed the towel aside and ran his fingers through the dark, damp strands of her hair. It smelled like freshly cut watermelon. And she tasted as sweet as a Charleston Gray stolen from Jed Butterworth's melon patch. He sampled every inch of her, licking and probing with his tongue every intimate fold and curve of her body.

She was moaning when he finished—sprawled naked on her bed, wet from his mouth and begging him to come in. She didn't have to beg. He was more than ready himself. When he drove into her, it was like being sucked into a river's eddy, and he gave himself over to the power that pulled him into its center of spectacular pleasure, then spewed him out, spent, sated, prostrate.

"I missed you," he murmured, looking deeply into her eyes and touching her face lightly with his fingers. Such a beautiful face. Such beautiful eyes, their purple chased from the centers by the blackness of her newly satiated desire. She was a lover like no other he'd ever had. None. The thought brought a shadow of guilt on its tail. He ignored the guilt—easy to do with her skin still damp against his own and the lingering musk of their lovemaking arousing him again—and hugged her to him. "Lord, how I've missed you."

Carrie was like a drug, and he was addicted. *Susan, forgive me.* He kissed her again.

FRANK HAD TO GO to something at the school on Tuesday night, so late that afternoon, Carrie went by the bakery and picked up a dozen brownies and a dozen macaroons and went calling on Clyde Burrows.

The gate was locked, so she honked the horn and waited. The dogs came first. He soon came over the rise, shotgun tucked in the crook of his arm.

"Well, lookie here who's come," he said to the dogs. "I hope you've got something good in that box," he said to her.

"I do. Brownies and macaroons. And I brought a CD player and some CDs, though I hoped you and I might do some singing on our own."

"We might." He opened the gate. "Come on up to the house. I just made a pot of coffee. You had supper? I've got some fresh fried squirrel and greens."

Carrie fought a shudder. "Thanks, but I planned to fill up on brownies instead of having supper."

Clyde grinned. "Not partial to squirrel, are you?"

She laughed. "You don't miss much, do you?"

"Not much."

They sat on the porch and drank bitter coffee and ate brownies and macaroons and watched the sun set and the evening sky go gray. They sang all of Waylon Jennings, Willie Nelson and George Straits's best songs and even one or two Garth Brooks numbers and an old Hank Williams hit that Uncle Tuck used to sing around the ranch. Clyde's horny fingers moved deftly over the guitar strings as he sang in a strong baritone voice with a bit of a whiskey edge to it. He'd start the words to one tune and she'd join in, then she'd start the next one.

They harmonized perfectly. Their voices echoed through the pine boughs and brought out the stars. They sang the moon up, then finally stopped when the night's chill made her nose numb.

"It's late," she said. "I have to go. This has been fun."

"Come back anytime."

"Thanks. I bought the CD player and the CDs as a gift for you. Your deciding to sign the oil lease made my job a lot easier, and I appreciate it."

"Like I said, you tickled my fancy right off. You've got spirit. And you're a pretty fair singer, too. Let me get the lantern, and I'll walk you to the gate."

On the way to her car, Carrie said, "Have you bought that new pickup yet?"

"Not yet. Figured I'd wait till I got the money in my hands. When did you say that show was?"

"The Fall Follies? It's Saturday night at the high school auditorium. Are you coming?"

He shrugged. "Never can tell. You going to be leaving town soon?"

"Yes. I'll probably have things wrapped up by the middle of next week."

"Hate to see you go. Heard talk that Frank Outlaw was sweet on you. Thought he might be anxious for you to stay in Naconiche."

"Nope. He hasn't mentioned it."

And he hadn't. Frank knew her work was winding down. They'd discussed it only last night. Never once had he even hinted at wanting to see her again after she left. That stung a little.

No, it stung a lot—because for all her protestations to the contrary, Carrie had finally admitted to herself that it would be very easy to fall in love with Frank Outlaw.

## Chapter Seventeen

The week seemed to fly by in a blur of work, rehearsals, stolen moments with Frank—and even a football game. Before Carrie knew it, Saturday morning had arrived, and the cast had assembled for final rehearsal before the show that night.

"I want to thank all of you for the hard work you've put in," Nonie Outlaw said as she addressed those gathered in the auditorium. "And to show our appreciation, the committee is sponsoring a cast party at the Twilight Tearoom tonight after the performance. You'll be happy to know that our ticket sales have surpassed last year's, and we have standing room only."

The crowd cheered, and Barry and his assistant directors took over for the last run-through. It was a bit chaotic, but things went reasonably well. The "Diamonds" number was flawless, and Sonny and Cher drew lots of laughs and a big round of applause from those still in the auditorium when the sixties came up. Carrie figured that they would really knock 'em dead in their full costumes that night.

She and Frank left after the sixties segment and decided to go to Travis Lake for Chinese. J.J. and

Mary Beth had taken the kids with them earlier. They were going to see new baby goats somewhere.

"This had been a busy week for you," Frank said as they drove.

"Very. Almost all the contracts for the local people are signed. I've contacted the majority of out-of-town owners, and their papers are in the mail. My business here should be finished by Tuesday or Wednesday." Watching his expression carefully, she held her breath, waiting for him to make some response to her leaving.

Was that a tiny clenching of his jaw? She couldn't be sure. He didn't take his eyes from the road. "Where will you be going next?"

"Oklahoma, I think."

"I see."

*I see. What kind of response is that?* she wanted to yell at him. But she didn't. Since he still wore his gold wedding ring, it was obvious where his heart was. Despite the passion, despite all their common interests and the fun they had together, Carrie had to accept that Frank wasn't interested in any kind of long-term relationship with her. And she'd fished around, giving him several opportunities in the past week to ask her to stay longer or at least indicate some interest in their seeing each other in the future. He hadn't taken the bait. He'd said nothing. Nada.

But since when had she become so shy? If she wanted to know his feelings, why didn't she ask?

Simple. She was afraid to hear his answer.

*Chicken.*

"You're awfully quiet," Frank said.

"I was just thinking."

"About what?"

She screwed up her courage and almost crossed her fingers in a childish gesture. It was put up or shut up time. "I was just thinking that I'm going to miss Naconiche and all the people I've met here. I'm going to miss you, Your Honor, something awful. I don't like to even consider the possibility that we might never see each other again.

If that wasn't the perfect opening, she didn't know what was.

He didn't say anything for about a week. Her stomach turned over twice.

"I'm going to miss you, too." Then he smiled. "And I don't think anybody in town will forget you in that little black costume you modeled for me. I know I won't."

*Damn!* So much for fishing expeditions.

"We're going to early church tomorrow," Frank said. "Want to come over and go riding about ten-thirty? It's supposed to rain tomorrow afternoon. We could grill outside if the weather holds."

"Sure. I won't pass up a chance to ride Betsy."

She smiled, but Carrie felt a horrible ache in her chest. Somewhere along the way, her idea of having a brief affair with Frank with no strings attached had backfired. The closer her departure date came, the more she realized that, while she wasn't looking, she'd come perilously close to falling in love with Frank Outlaw.

More than perilously close.

She was over the edge.

And she couldn't believe that she was beginning to think of her nomadic job as a royal pain. She'd always loved the excitement of it—just as she'd always loved the excitement of Houston. Yet, several times lately she'd found herself daydreaming about settling down in Naconiche. What kind of goofy idea was that? Were her hormones out of whack or something?

It was crazy. Those coupling-nesting instincts would pass. She wasn't about to get on that marriage merry-go-round that her mother rode—even if Frank was interested in a future with her.

Which he wasn't.

*Enjoy the moment and move on,* she told herself.

THAT NIGHT, toward the end of the intermission between the thirties and forties segments, Carrie and Kelly stood backstage and peeked out a hole in the curtain at the audience. The two of them were dressed in their scanty black costumes, which were nothing more than satin bathing suits with lapels, black fishnets and high heels. They had on their long black gloves and tons of the cheap rhinestone jewelry Kelly had bought.

Kelly had been so taken with the Sonny and Cher hairpieces Carrie had bought in Houston that Kelly dug up a couple of platinum-blond wigs for them that would rival any that Dolly Parton owned. The top hats wouldn't fit over the curled and fluffed blonde tresses, so the hats were abandoned, but they kept the canes.

"Looks like everybody in town turned out," Kelly said, one eye to the hole. "Good Lord! Is that Clyde Burrows?"

"Where?"

"On the aisle, sixth row back." Kelly stepped aside so that Carrie could peep out the flap.

Carrie smiled when she saw him. His gray hair was slicked back in a short ponytail and his beard appeared to have been trimmed. "Yep. That's him, all right. And I don't think he brought his shotgun or his dogs.''

The lights flashed.

''Forties people, take your places,'' Barry said.

Carrie and Kelly moved to the wings while the Andrews sisters and the others hurried to their spots.

After the forties performances, the stage went dark, that group exited and the fifties bunch assembled while the narrator did his part. When the spotlight came up on Kelly and Carrie, a murmur went through the auditorium—along with a whistle or two.

*Uh-oh,* Carrie thought, *we're sunk.* But as soon as they started their number, the audience burst into spontaneous applause. They laughed at a suggestive bump of the hips and scrambled to catch the ''diamonds'' she and Kelly threw to the crowd. She tossed two bracelets in the area where Clyde was sitting and hoped he caught one.

When they ended their song with a suggestive wiggle and wink, everybody went wild. They ran off the stage, but Barry stopped them before Carrie could jerk off her wig and had them go back for another bow.

The clapping and whistling grew louder as they reappeared, bowed and tossed the rest of their jewelry to the audience with blown kisses.

When they ran off the second time, Kelly said, ''Wow. Heady stuff.''

Carrie laughed and pulled off her wig as they hurried to the dressing room for her change. ''Makes you giddy, doesn't it?''

Once the door was closed, Carrie handed her gloves and cane to Kelly, stepped out of her heels and peeled off the satin outfit. While she was putting on her bell-bottoms, Kelly held the blouse ready and slipped it over her head. She slid her feet into sandals, and while Kelly buckled the straps, Carrie put on the long black wig and secured it with pins. She traded her rhinestone earrings for big hoops and ran a pale pink lip wand over her mouth.

Carrie held out her arms. "How's this?"

"Sensational. Cher's mother couldn't tell the difference. Don't forget your vest."

Frank had fashioned a curly fleece vest for her that matched the one he'd made from the lining of an old jacket. She put it on. "Thanks for helping, Kelly," she said over her shoulder as she yanked open the door.

Frank was waiting outside. He grinned when he saw her. She did some grinning of her own. His wig was a riot. And he'd dug up a fake mustache from somewhere.

"Catch your breath. We have plenty of time. You and Kelly were dynamite."

"Thanks. I was afraid we might have given her minister a heart attack."

He chuckled. "I think he clapped the loudest. Ready?"

She took a deep breath, and they walked to the wings just as the last act of the fifties segment ended.

If the "Diamonds" number had brought the house down, their Sonny and Cher impersonation absolutely stole the show. People laughed uproariously as they sang, "I Got You Babe." They applauded until Carrie and Frank did an encore—which was merely a repeat of the chorus. It hadn't occurred to them to plan anything else.

When they came offstage later, a gangly teenager was waiting with a big bouquet of red roses and baby's breath tied with a huge red bow. "These are for you, Miss Campbell," he said, handing them to Carrie and grinning slyly at Frank. "From an admirer."

Her brows went up as she took the flowers into her arms. She nuzzled the blossoms. "Oh, they're beautiful, and they smell heavenly. Thank you, Frank."

"Sorry, but they're not from me," he said. "Wish I'd thought of it."

Puzzled, she looked for a card and found one tied to a stem.

*Congratulations!* the card said. *From your friend Clyde.*

Carrie laughed out loud and hugged the bouquet to her.

"Who are they from?" Frank asked.

She gave him a saucy wink. "From an admirer."

AFTER THEY CHANGED, Frank and Carrie were watching the rest of the show from the wings when Wes Outlaw came up and whispered something to Frank. They spoke in hushed tones for a moment, then Wes left. Frank looked distracted.

"Something wrong?" Carrie asked.

"Janey's not feeling well. Tummy ache from too much excitement I imagine. Matilda is off this weekend, and Dad offered to take the kids home and stay, but I'd better go. Janey's asking for me. Looks like I'll have to miss the cast party."

"Is there anything I can do?"

He shook his head. "I'm sure it's nothing serious. Sorry I have to leave, but I'll see you in the morning."

Carrie watched the rest of the show and clapped as

loudly as anybody when the final curtain dropped. This had been such fun. After she gathered her things and went outside, she found Clyde Burrows waiting for her. He wore a white shirt and dark pants, and his shoes were shined.

"You were really good," he said.

"Thanks. And thank you so much for the roses." She hugged them to her face. "They're beautiful."

"You're mighty welcome."

"I'm glad you came tonight."

"Me, too. Enjoyed myself. I didn't know Millie had a voice like that."

"She's something, isn't she?"

Clyde shuffled his feet awkwardly. "Well, I'd best be gettin' along. I just wanted to tell you how much I enjoyed myself."

He'd turned and started to leave when an idea popped into Carrie's head. "Wait! How would you like to go to a party with me?"

"A party?"

"Yep. A cast party."

"But...I'm not part of—"

"You'd be my guest. Tell you what, we can be the entertainment. Go home and get your guitar and meet me at the Twilight Tearoom. Know where that is?"

"Guess I do. Go by it every time I drive to town."

She smiled. "Then I'll see you there in a few minutes."

ELLEN AND DIXIE were putting out cookies and sandwiches when Carrie arrived at the tearoom, where a crowd had already gathered. "Need any help?" she asked them.

"No, we've about got it licked," Ellen said. "You

were great tonight. I thought Frank was a scream in that wig.''

''Wasn't he? And I enjoyed your flapper number. Y'all were really good.''

''Except for me,'' Dixie said. ''I was out of step the whole time.''

''I didn't notice,'' Carrie said. It was only a tiny lie.

Kelly waved from across the room and headed toward the refreshment table. She was beaming, and her eyes were bright. ''You wouldn't believe the comments I've had on our act,'' she said. ''Where's Frank?''

''He had to go home. Janey wasn't feeling well.''

''Bummer,'' Ellen said.

''Holy cow!'' Dixie said. ''Would you look who just came in the door.''

Carrie glanced over her shoulder and grinned at the man who stood there looking as if he might bolt at any minute. ''Clyde Burrows. He's my date.''

As she made her way to the door, several people complimented her on her performances, and she returned the compliments. By the time she reached Clyde, he was acting as nervous as a hooker in church.

''Hey, Clyde,'' Carrie said, slipping her arm through his. ''Come on over to the refreshment table. I didn't see any macaroons, but the pecan sandies looked good.''

''I'm not sure this is a good idea,'' he said. ''Maybe I'd best go on home.''

''Nope,'' she said, taking his guitar by the neck and guiding him through the crowd. She laid the guitar on the bar and led him to the food.

J.J. and Miss Nonie were filling their plates when they walked up, and Miss Nonie tried not to seem startled at seeing Clyde.

"Clyde's my guest," she told them. "He brought his guitar, and we thought we might entertain the entertainers at the party."

"Why…why…that's a wonderful gesture," Miss Nonie said. "Thank you. I didn't know you played the guitar, Clyde."

"Yes, ma'am, I play a little. You put on a fine show tonight, Miss Nonie."

"Wasn't everybody wonderful? Here, have a chicken salad sandwich, Clyde. I made these myself."

After they'd schmoozed a while—and saying that Clyde schmoozed was stretching a point—they hoisted themselves onto the bar, and Clyde picked up his guitar. Everybody was talking and laughing, and nobody paid them any attention.

"Are you sure this is a good idea?" he asked.

"Positive. Let's start with 'I'm in the Jailhouse Now.'"

Clyde shrugged and began strumming. By the time they'd sung the first verse, the conversation had died in a ripple effect and every eye in the place was on them.

By the time they finished, everybody was clapping and singing along. They went immediately into "Friends in Low Places," and the room rocked. They played two requests, then Clyde laid his guitar aside and they begged off singing another.

Carrie had never seen so much back-slapping as Clyde received, and he was grinning like a kid who'd won the spelling bee.

"I never would have figured that Clyde Burrows could sing and play like that," J.J. said.

"He's great," Mary Beth added.

"Isn't he?" Carrie said. "He plays the banjo, too."

"Mama will have him signed up for next year's Follies before he leaves," J.J. said.

Carrie snagged another chocolate chip cookie and chatted with Barry and two of the assistant directors.

"I understand you won't be with us next year," Barry said.

"Right. I'll be leaving town next week," she told him.

"A shame. You're a natural for our productions."

"I'm a natural-born ham, you mean."

Barry laughed. "I'm a ham, too. I freely admit it. Performing gets in the blood, and there's no high like walking onto a stage. If you can arrange it, drop around at the end of next October."

"Who knows? I might do that."

The party started breaking up a few minutes later, and Clyde, guitar in hand, came over to her. He was still beaming.

"Thanks for the invite, Carrie," he said. "I ain't had so much fun since the hogs ate Sister." He cackled.

"I'm glad you came." She walked to the door with him, then outside.

"Where's your feller?"

"What feller?"

"The judge."

"Oh, Frank's little girl got sick." She stuck out her hand. "In case I don't see you again before I go, Clyde, meeting you and doing business has been a pleasure. Thank you."

He took her hand. "No, I thank *you,* Miss Carrie Campbell. You've done a right smart for me." He pumped her hand again, then turned and strode off.

Gosh, she was going to miss that old codger.

And a couple of dozen others she could name.

The party at the Twilight Tearoom had been a hundred times more fun than the big blowout a week before in Houston.

Maybe it was because the people here really cared about each other. She was going to miss that, too.

THE NEXT MORNING Carrie had just had her first cup of coffee when the phone rang.

"I've got an emergency," Frank said in a tone that almost stopped her heart. "My older brother Cole has been shot, and he's in surgery in Houston. It's serious. J.J. is already on his way there with Mom and Dad, and I'm trying to get away to go, too, but I have a problem."

"How may I help?" Carrie asked.

"I can't leave the kids alone, and Matilda isn't due back until two this afternoon. I don't have time to try to find a sitter. Would you mind staying with them until Matilda comes?"

"Of course not. I'll be right there."

Carrie threw on her clothes, grabbed her brush and cosmetics bag and hurried out to her car. She could tame her hair and put on makeup later.

She broke speed limits getting to Frank's place. As she rumbled over the cattle guard, she could see his car sitting out front with the motor running, the thick plume from his exhaust billowing into the damp, chilly gloom. When she pulled up beside his car, he and the twins were waiting at the front door. The kids were in their pajamas, and Frank wore dress slacks and a sport coat. Janey had her arms wrapped around one of his legs.

"I really appreciate this," Frank said.

"No problem. Just be careful driving. It's a dreary morning, and the wind's up. I don't think the rain will hold off until afternoon. How is Janey feeling? Any special instructions?"

He stroked Janey's hair. "She's feeling much better this morning, aren't you, sweetheart? They've just had breakfast, and I promised them that after they got dressed you would play a game with them. Okay?"

"Sure. If they promise not to beat me too badly." She winked at the twins.

Jimmy grinned a grin amazingly like his father's. Janey giggled.

Frank kissed everybody goodbye, including Carrie, though hers was no more than the same peck the children received.

"The kids can show you where things are, and there's plenty in the refrigerator for lunch," Frank said. "The cat and kittens are in the laundry room. Buster, the dog, is still at the vet after his surgery. Ask Matilda to pick him up tomorrow. Tell Matilda that I'll call later this afternoon when I know something. I have a bag in the car in case I have to stay overnight. I need to get going."

"Don't worry about a thing," she said. "We'll be just fine."

They stood in the doorway and waved as Frank drove away.

He was barely past the cattle guard when it started raining and Janey threw up on Carrie's foot.

## Chapter Eighteen

Janey was upset; Carrie was upset. Jimmy just said, "Ewwww. I'm going to watch cartoons."

Carrie grabbed Jimmy's shirttail before he darted away. "Not yet. I need some help. Would you bring me some paper towels, please?"

"I can't reach them."

"Try."

Jimmy trudged off at a snail's pace.

"*Hurry,* please."

"I'm going to be sick again," Janey said.

Carrie quickly herded her out the front door, trying to make it to the edge of the porch.

They didn't quite make it.

This time Carrie's other foot got it.

Lightning flashed, thunder rolled and wind flailed hundred-year-old trees as if they were mere bushes. As rain began pouring down in huge driving sheets, Janey started to wail. "You hate me."

"Don't cry, honey. I don't hate you. You can't help it if you're sick."

"I've ruined your shoes." Janey bawled louder.

"They're only sneakers. I can wash them."

Jimmy returned with two sections of paper towels, one in each hand.

"That's not quite enough, sport. Bring me some more."

"There isn't any more. The thing is empty. I'm going to go watch *Jonny Quest*."

"Not yet. Bring me some regular towels. Hurry."

"I don't have to do what you say," Jimmy informed her. "You're not my mother."

"No, I'm not your mother by any stretch of the imagination, but I'm the supervising adult in this house," she said sternly. "You *will* do what I say or suffer serious consequences. Is that clear?"

Jimmy's eyes grew wide. "Yes, ma'am." He turned and ran.

"I'm going to do it again!" shrieked Janey.

This time they made it to the edge of the porch.

Carrie held one of the paper sheets out in the torrent pouring off the roof, wrung it out and bathed Janey's face. "Feeling better?"

She nodded. Jimmy came running out with an armload of blue-striped towels. Carrie wet the end of one of them and cleaned up Jancy.

"Is your tummy settled down now?"

"I think so," Janey said. "But my mouth tastes bad, and I'm thirsty."

"I'll get you a glass of water," Jimmy said.

"It's not a good idea to drink anything now, but we'll brush your teeth. That will help. Sit right there on the swing until I clean up a little."

Gingerly, Carrie removed her shoes, tossed them onto the steps for nature to wash and rolled up her pant legs. Holding on to the porch post, she stuck out one foot then the other under the downpour. The rainwater was cold. When she had dried her feet, she quickly cleaned up the messes as best she could and tossed the towels out into the yard.

A huge bolt of lightning flashed and cracked, and the ground shook.

Janey shrieked. "I'm scared," she whined.

Jimmy looked pale, but he said, "Nothing to be scared of. It's just an old thunderstorm."

"Right," Carrie told them. "And it's getting cold out here. Let's go inside and snuggle up and watch cartoons."

After Carrie helped Janey brush her teeth, she got her settled beside Jimmy on the couch in the den—with a plastic bucket nearby—and went in search of the master bedroom. She felt guilty rummaging around in Frank's room and in his chest of drawers, but her feet were freezing and she needed to find a dry pair of socks. She found more than she bargained for.

A radiant bride in an ornate gold frame smiled down from the wall above the chest. A smaller eight-by-ten of the same woman holding two babies sat on the nightstand beside his bed.

Susan. She was lovely. Carrie didn't take time to study the photographs carefully, nor to think much about their prominent display. Their meaning was obvious. Frank was still very connected to his dead wife. Any smattering of hope for a future with him vanished. Grabbing a pair of Frank's white socks, she tried her best to ignore Susan's mocking smile and called Kelly from the bedside phone.

"I was just leaving to deliver a baby," Kelly said. "What's up?"

"Bottom line, I'm sitting for Janey and Jimmy Outlaw, and Janey has been throwing up. Three times already. The housekeeper is off and Frank's on his way to Houston. I know nothing about kids. What do I do?''

''It's probably the stomach flu that's been going around. Keep her quiet. Feed her a few ice chips, if she can tolerate them, until she can hold down a little Gatorade, and don't let her eat barbecued ribs.''

''Very funny, Doctor.''

''Sorry. Does she have any fever?''

''I don't know. I don't think so.''

''Check it, and I'll call you later. Just use common sense. Clear liquids, Jell-O. Maybe a cracker later. Gotta go. This baby won't wait.''

After a thorough search of the house, Carrie finally located a thermometer in the middle drawer of Frank's bathroom. She washed it in alcohol, then hot water and took it to the den. ''Open your mouth and stick this under your tongue,'' she told Janey.

''Why don't we use the one that goes in your ear?'' Janey asked.

''In your ear?''

''Yeah,'' Jimmy said. ''That's what Daddy and Matilda use. I'll get it.''

He was back in a moment with a box. Thank goodness the directions were inside.

Ninety-nine point two. She took it again to be sure. There was only a tenth of a degree difference. *Not too bad,* Carrie thought. Only the body doing its job fighting the bug. After tucking a throw around Janey, Carrie went into the kitchen to wash her hands and crack some ice.

Rain hitting the kitchen windows sounded like sleet against the panes, and the sky was ominously dark.

The wind howled and whipped the trees fiercely. This was a serious storm. She'd better find some candles and kerosene lamps in case they lost power. And lay in some firewood.

After she'd fed Janey a bit of ice, she asked Jimmy to help her locate things, and soon she had several candlesticks and candles, three flashlights and two lamps on the bar. Thank heavens plenty of wood was stacked under the patio cover outside, and she went ahead and started a fire. It would be cozy in any case.

"I'm hungry," Jimmy said.

"Me, too," Janey echoed.

"I'll find you a snack in a minute, Jimmy, but you can't have any food yet, Janey. We can try a little Gatorade."

"I want a hot dog with mustard and catsup and a dill pickle," Jimmy said.

"I'm gonna be sick again!"

Carrie made a dive for the bucket, but the wave passed and Janey didn't need it. She suspected that Jimmy's recitation of his gastronomic desires made his sister queasy. It did her.

"I can fix it," Jimmy said, marching into the kitchen.

"Fine. I'll try to find some Gatorade for Janey."

She found two kinds in the pantry and located other possible foodstuffs while she was there. There were saltines, soup and bouillon cubes, as well as packages of flavored gelatin. She set out a couple of packages to make up and poured some orange drink over ice cubes for Janey while Jimmy dragged a step stool over to the microwave and stuck a weiner inside.

"Are you supposed to be using that?" she asked.

Jimmy looked insulted. "I'm not a baby. I know how."

She shrugged and took the glass to Janey.

"Sip slowly," Carrie told the child, "and see how it feels in your tummy."

Janey took two slow sips. "That's all I want right now."

"Fine. You just watch cartoons and—"

There was an explosion in the kitchen.

Rushing to see what happened, Carrie knocked over the plastic bucket and stubbed her toe on the coffee table. Cursing under her breath, she limped to the microwave where Jimmy stood on the step stool, a stricken look on his face.

"What happened?" she cried.

"The weenie blew up."

Shriveling fragments of the ill-fated hot dog were still going around on the carousel—with twelve minutes to go on the timer. She jabbed the Off button. "I thought you said you knew how to use the microwave."

His mouth turned down and his chin trembled.

"Have you ever used it before?"

A tear rolled down his cheek. "I'm not allowed."

"Now you know why. Get another weenie while I clean up the remains of this one."

While he made a trip to the fridge, she found a fresh roll of paper towels and disposed of the shrapnel.

When Jimmy returned with a weiner in his fist, Carrie ripped off a sheet of paper towel and put it on the counter. "Hot dog there." She pointed to the paper, then located a fork and handed it to him. "Climb up on the stool and give it a good poke with the fork.''

He followed her directions.

"Know why you stick it with the fork?"

He shook his head shyly.

"Because if you don't, when it cooks, it builds up steam that has nowhere to go.'' Carrie puffed up her cheeks and crossed her eyes. "Then—*kablooie!*'' She poked him in the tummy, and he laughed.

Carrie showed him how to roll the weiner in paper and put in on the carousel. "Now we have to decide how long to cook it. I think about twenty seconds. Do you know which one is a two?" He pointed correctly. "Right. And a zero?" He picked that one, too. "Okay. Punch the two, then the zero. Good job! I'll push the start button. Only grown-ups can push the start button, okay?''

He nodded.

"Know what would happen if you pushed two-zero-zero?''

"What?''

"It would turn into a petrified mess.''

"What's petrified?''

"Like a rock. And if you pushed some wrong buttons, it could cook until it became a charcoal lump and caught fire. Where are the buns?''

Jimmy went for buns while she dug mustard and catsup from the fridge. Together they fixed his hot dog and carried it to the table.

"Want chips?'' she asked.

"Yes. And a pickle.''

Carrie handed him the pickle jar and a fork, then made two kinds of gelatin and put them in the refrigerator to set.

While Jimmy ate, she went to check on Janey. "Feeling okay?"

"I'm hot."

Carrie felt Janey's forehead. She was burning up.

"Let me take your temperature, sweetie," Carrie said.

A hundred and two and a half. Her heart flew to her throat. This was getting serious.

She picked up the phone to call Kelly.

The line was dead. Her cell phone. Where was her cell phone? It was still in her bag in the car. Carrie ran to the front door and flung it open. She could hardly see through the fury of the rain. She'd be soaked to the skin the moment she set foot off the porch. She wouldn't melt, but these were the only clothes she had.

A raincoat. She needed a raincoat.

Wheeling around, she dashed back inside—and almost ran over Jimmy, who had followed her.

"Sorry, sport," she said dancing to one side. "Where does your dad keep his raincoat?"

Jimmy pointed to a closet in the entryway. She hurried to the closet and began frantically rummaging inside. She found parkas and other coats and jackets of various kinds, including two small yellow slickers, but no adult-size raincoat.

"Where? Where?" she shouted. "I can't find it!"

"He took it with him in the car."

"He *took* it?" she shrieked, clamping her arms over her head.

When she whirled around, his eyes were big and his chin was trembling again. She felt like pond scum. Kneeling down, she gathered him into her arms. "It's okay, honey. It's okay. I'm acting like a gooney bird.''

''I'm gonna be sick.''

She grabbed him and ran for the porch.

When nothing came up after a minute or two, she asked, ''Still feeling sick?''

He shook his head. ''I'm cold.''

And no wonder. The child still wore his pajamas.

''You run back inside with Janey and stay close to the bucket. I have to get my cell phone from my car. Okay?''

He nodded and went back into the house. If she got drenched or not, she had to retrieve that phone. Immediately.

She sprinted to the kitchen, snatched up two plastic grocery bags and ran back out to the entry hall. One bag she put on her head and tied under her chin, the other she stuffed inside the one on her head. She grabbed the only umbrella she could find—a small plastic one with fish on it.

Then she stepped out onto the porch and stripped. Down to the skin. Dropping her clothes beside a clean towel still on the swing, she opened the umbrella and made a mad dash for her car.

The umbrella was about the size of a hubcap, and the wind snatched it from her hand immediately and sent it flying over the trees. A huge bolt of lightning flashed and a deafening *crack* sounded nearby. A tree, she figured. She'd probably get electrocuted out in this mess, and then what would happen to the children?

Cursing the wind and the rain, she yanked open the car door. Leaning over with water pouring onto her lovely leather seats and icy sheets pelting her bare bottom, she pulled the extra plastic sack from beneath her headgear, stuffed her bag into it and tied it securely.

Clutching the bag against her, she hunched down, splashed back through the horrendous downpour and ran up the steps.

Jimmy and Janey stood in the doorway—bug-eyed.

"You're nekkid!" Jimmy said.

"Tell me something I don't know," she yelled, her teeth chattering like skeletons dancing on a tin roof. "Inside! Now! Scoot!"

They scooted. She ripped the grocery sack off her head, grabbed a towel from the swing and began rubbing her body vigorously. Her feet were numb and her goose bumps had sprouted babies. She was chilled to the bone, beside herself with concern about Janey, and now the twins had watched her whole nude rain romp.

If she were in Bowen County, they would probably throw her in jail for lewd behavior with minors. Frank would in all likelihood be furious. But hell's bells, the twins were only five. Surely they weren't traumatized. Besides, most of the essentials were covered with the sack she held.

Dammit, she was doing the best she could—and it was too late to worry about the episode now.

As soon as she was dressed, she fished her bag out of the wet plastic sack and hurried inside, eager to stand by the fire.

The lights were out.

"The 'lectricity's off," Jimmy said, shining a flashlight in her eyes.

Fending off the glare, she said, "I noticed." Still seeing spots from the afterimage, she felt her way to the bar and lit some candles and the kerosene lamps. She set one of the lamps on the mantel over the fireplace.

Back to the warm flames, she dug her phone out of her bag. The twins sat side by side on the couch staring at her. She waggled her finger at them. "If you tell a soul about this, I will hang you by your toes on the clothesline and throw sardines at you."

They only giggled.

She punched in Kelly's number, and her friend answered on the first ring. She was still at the hospital.

"I've been trying to reach you," Kelly said.

"Phone's out, and I just got my cell from my car. The power is out, too." Carrie explained the situation with Janey's fever. "Should I try to bring her in to the hospital?"

"Heavens no," Kelly said. "I doubt if you could get through anyhow. I understand that the creek between you and the highway is over the bridge, and there are trees down everywhere. I'm pretty sure that Janey has the twenty-four hour virus that's going around." She explained how to bring down the fever and gave general directions for care.

"I suppose it's too much to hope that Matilda will show up this afternoon."

"I wouldn't count on it, Carrie. Things are really bad outside, and this front has stalled. It won't be letting up for several hours. I'll call the sheriff's department and tell them that you're safe so that you can save your phone battery. Check in with me about midafternoon—sooner if you need me."

MATILDA DIDN'T SHOW UP at two. Or at four. According to the battery-powered radio Jimmy had found, there were travel advisories because of flooding, and power was out in a large area of their part of the county.

Janey's fever went down, and she didn't throw up anymore. Praise be, Jimmy didn't get sick. Carrie kept wood on the fire, and after she and Jimmy gathered all the quilts and blankets and pillows into the den, she closed off the rest of the house to retain heat, leaving open the door to the laundry room where the new kittens were. Carrie considered moving their box into the den, but they seemed snug enough where they were.

There was no shortage of food in the kitchen, though some of their meals were quite creative. She'd found a big iron pot with a lid and had boiled water in the fireplace to add to dry soup—the clear part going to Janey and the noodles and chicken going to Jimmy and her.

The kids actually thought it was great fun to camp out in the den. They played games and sang songs. The twins taught her "I'm a Little Teapot" and she taught them "Mama, Don't Let Your Babies Grow Up to Be Cowboys."

The rain slowed during the afternoon and stopped by seven o'clock. She turned on her phone and called Kelly again.

Kelly had talked to one of the deputies in J.J.'s office and had messages to relay. Matilda was stuck at her sister's house until at least tomorrow. Cole Outlaw, Frank and J.J.'s older brother, had made it through surgery okay and was in stable condition. J.J. and his parents were going to stay in Houston for a while, but Frank said he would be home as soon as he could. Probably tomorrow morning.

"Are you going to be okay?" Kelly asked.

"We're doing just fine," Carrie said. "Gotta go. We're toasting marshmallows and making raspberry tea."

"I'm not sure Janey should be having marshmallows."

"Jimmy's having marshmallows. Janey and Barbie and I are having tea. Talk to you later."

By nine o'clock, Carrie was worn out. She knew the kids had to be. "Bedtime," she announced.

The kids groused, begging to play another game or sing another song, but their eyes definitely looked droopy.

"Nope. I'm pooped. Let's make our bed right here by the fire, and I'll tell you a story."

After she stirred the embers and added extra logs, she and Jimmy made a big quilt pallet on the floor and piled pillows at one end. Everybody made a last visit to the bathroom, and she doused the candles and one kerosene lamp. The other lamp she turned low, and each twin had a flashlight.

She got in the middle and drew up the pair of fleecy blankets she'd set aside for cover. Janey and Jimmy snuggled up close to her, and Carrie told them the story of Snow White and the Seven Dwarfs—what she could remember of it. They even sang the "Hi-Ho" song from the movie. And when she couldn't remember the names of all the dwarfs, Jimmy supplied them.

When she finished the story, the twins were still and their breathing even. Asleep, she thought.

Then a tiny hand touched her cheek. "I love you," Janey whispered.

Tears sprang to Carrie's eyes. "I love you, too."

Jimmy burrowed closer. "Me, too," he murmured very softly.

She gently kissed his forehead and breathed his little boy smell. "Me, too."

When had that happened? When had she lost her heart to these two little imps? Would wonders never cease?

IT WAS ALMOST DAYLIGHT when Frank finally got home. The creek was down enough to pass by four o'clock that morning, but the crew hadn't finished removing the tree across the road until after five o'clock.

The house was quiet when he let himself in the front door. Only the cat met him with a silent stitch of her tail. He moved into the den and saw the glowing embers of a fire and the dim light from a kerosene lamp on the mantel.

Then he saw them bundled in covers on the floor. Carrie was in the middle with an arm around each of the twins, and they were snuggled as close to her as they could get. They looked like three angels.

A lump came in his throat.

He sat down on the couch and watched them until he fell asleep.

# Chapter Nineteen

By ten o'clock Wednesday morning, Carrie decided that she couldn't put it off any longer. She packed, loaded her belongings into her car and strapped Monroe into the passenger seat. After one last check of her room, she took the key to the office.

Will glanced up from the magazine he was reading, then hopped up when he saw her. "You really leavin'?"

"As soon as I pay my bill."

"Got it right here. Sure hate to see you go. It was nice having you in town. And I won't deny that having that oil lease money won't ease my life considerable."

"Thanks, Will. Say goodbye to all the guys for me."

"I'll do it."

She settled her bill and headed for her car. Mary Beth waved to her from the front door of the tearoom and trotted over.

"I wish you were staying," Mary Beth said, giving her a hug. "You've become a friend—and I was hoping that we might become family."

Carrie only smiled and shrugged. "Tell J.J. good-bye for me. And Dixie and Ellen and the others."

"I will. Do come back for our wedding."

"I'll try."

They both knew she probably wouldn't.

A gigantic lump clogged her throat as Carrie got in her car and drove away from the Twilight Inn.

She'd said most of her goodbyes the day before—to Kelly, Clyde, Janey and Jimmy. She'd enjoyed one last bittersweet ride on Betsy, then she and Frank had gone to Travis Lake for dinner. Neither of them had eaten much.

He'd rented a nice motel room for a few hours, and their lovemaking had been almost desperate. It had been on the tip of her tongue to tell him that she loved him, but she didn't. It wouldn't have done any good. He was in love with a ghost.

Instead, when he'd driven her to her room about midnight, she'd kissed him one last time and whispered, "I'm going to miss you something fierce."

He'd simply clutched her to him and hadn't said a word.

That had hurt.

She drove around the square, saying a silent farewell to the little hick town she'd come to love, waving to a person here and there, including the sassy little waitress, who was sweeping the sidewalk in front of the City Grill. The Double Dip was closed. Miss Nonie and Wes were still in Houston with Cole, who remained in intensive care.

With one last glance to the second floor of the courthouse, Carrie sighed and turned onto the street that would take her by the library. She dropped a

novel that she never got to finish in the book slot,
then drove by the JP's office on her way out of town.

*Rest in peace, Horace P. Pfannepatter.*


"I WANT SOME RASPBERRY TEA!" Janey said at
breakfast on Friday morning.

"We don't have any raspberry tea," Matilda said.
"The choices are orange juice or apple juice."

"Carrie fixed raspberry tea for me," Janey whined.
"It made my tummy feel good."

Janey seemed to be whining most of the time,
Frank thought. And Jimmy went around dragging his
feet and staring at the floor. Carrie's name came up
frequently.

"Maybe she brought it with her because I can't find
hide nor hair of any raspberry tea."

"It's in the pantry," Jimmy said. "I'll show you."
He hopped up from the table, went to the pantry and
came back with a package of raspberry gelatin.
"This." He plunked it on the table.

"But that's Jell-O," Frank said.

"When the 'lectricity went off, and it wouldn't
make," Janey explained, "Carrie said we could just
drink it like tea cause it was gonna melt in our stom-
achs anyhow."

"Makes a perverted kind of sense," Frank said.

"What's preverted?" Jimmy asked.

"*Per*verted. It's…uh…twisted or strange."

"Like when Carrie ran around nekkid in the rain."
Coffee spewed from Frank's mouth.

"You weren't supposed to tell that!" Janey yelled.
"She didn't want anybody to think she was a prev-
ert."

Matilda looked as though she might faint.

"I love Carrie," Janey said. "I wish she hadn't gone off and left us. Now I'll never have a mommy." She ran from the table in tears.

Frank went after Janey, trying his best to comfort her—and get the whole story about Carrie being naked in the rain. When he finally pieced the truth together, he chuckled and hugged his daughter. "I understand emergencies. Carrie was very brave to go out into the storm for the phone. Nobody thinks she's a pervert."

"I miss her," Janey said.

Damn! He missed Carrie, too.

SEEMED THAT everybody missed Carrie. He'd heard the sentiment voiced a dozen times or more since she left. And most of the people who mentioned it looked at him as if it were his fault that she left. J.J. was the most vocal about his feelings.

"You're a damned fool. You ought to have your butt kicked from here to Amarillo for letting Carrie get away," J.J. said at lunch that day. "Did you even ask her to stay?"

Frank shook his head.

"For Pete's sake, why not? Everybody in town knew you were crazy about her. And you're like a bear with a sore paw now that she's gone."

"Could we talk about something else?"

J.J. wouldn't let it go. "Have you even called her since she left?"

"No. Are you going to have some pie?"

J.J. snorted and gave up.

Frank had thought about calling Carrie, but what would he say? What could he offer? He wasn't ready. He just wasn't ready.

He figured that he'd get over her soon enough. After all, he hadn't known her all that long. Trying to rationalize his feelings, he told himself a lot of stuff, but the truth was that Carrie's leaving had ripped a hole in his heart and he was hurting.

It was pure hell.

WEDNESDAY AFTERNOON, Frank took a bouquet of yellow flowers to the cemetery. It was late and growing dark when he reached Susan's grave. He hadn't been there in a while.

He'd dreamed about Susan the night before. She was wearing a yellow dress and standing on the deck of a big ship waving to him. She looked radiant as she blew kisses and called, "Goodbye."

Frank had never paid much attention to dreams, but he woke up with the strangest sensation that he'd really seen Susan and she was trying to tell him something. The feeling had nagged him all day.

He put the bouquet of lilies by her headstone and stood listening as if she might talk to him and tell him what to do.

The only sound was the distant *whoosh* as cars passed on the highway.

"Susan, I can't go on like this. I loved you with all my heart and soul, but you're gone now and nothing can bring you back. It's time for me to let you go and get on with my life."

As soon as the words left his mouth a sudden peace settled over him. The feeling wrapped him in a cocoon of contentment, and his heart swelled in his chest. He'd made the right decision. Susan was giving him her blessing. Strange as it seemed, Frank *knew* that was what she'd been telling him. It was time to let her go.

He basked in that peacefulness for a few minutes, then he took off his wedding ring and put it in his pocket. "Goodbye, Susan." He turned and walked away.

He had to find Carrie and somehow convince her that she belonged in Naconiche with him.

CARRIE BLEW HER NOSE and put on a second pair of socks. The dump where she was staying was no Twilight Inn. The heat in her room wasn't working right, and the courthouse had been drafty to boot. She'd caught a cold trying to dig up information in this little section of Oklahoma.

Blast it, she hated this place. Just about every minute of every day she missed Naconiche—and Frank. She'd been so clever thinking that she was immune to loving and needing a man, so determined that she wasn't going to be like her mother that she'd forgotten some important things. Things like the basic needs of love and belonging and family.

Somewhere along the way, she'd not only fallen in love with Frank, she'd fallen in love with Janey and Jimmy. They were neat kids, and she figured that with a little practice, she would have made a darned good mother.

If she'd had the chance.

But she hadn't.

She wasn't the only one who had assumed that theirs would be a no-strings, short-term relationship. It seemed that Frank had the same agenda. Only for her, the rules had changed. She'd fallen in love. For the first time.

But that was over and done with, and she planned to move on with her life. She'd survived rejections before.

Carrie blew her nose again and told herself to get a grip.

She was just taking a cup of chicken broth from the microwave when there was a knock at the door. Hopefully, it was the maintenance man to fix the heat. She'd called twice.

But when she flung open the door, her caller wasn't the one she expected.

Judge Frank Outlaw stood there instead.

Stunned, she couldn't think of a thing to say. A barrage of emotions assaulted her. She wanted to throw herself into his arms and weep, but she didn't want to make a fool of herself again. She was just getting over the damage to her heart from their last encounter.

That was a lie. She hadn't gotten over anything. Her heart was still in shreds.

"Aren't you going to ask me in?" he said.

"Sure. Come in." She stepped aside.

"It's like an iceberg in here."

She sneezed. "Tell me something I don't know. How did you find me?"

"I called your uncle."

"He didn't tell me."

"I asked him not to."

"Why?"

"I wanted to surprise you."

"Okay," she said. "I'm surprised. Why are you here?"

"To tell you something that I didn't say before."

"And what's that?" she asked, trying to act disinterested.

"That I love you, Carrie Campbell."

Was she hallucinating? Had she turned feverish and imagined this whole episode? She glanced at his left hand. His wedding ring was gone. "You love me?"

"I do. More than I ever imagined I could love anyone. And I've missed you something fierce."

"That's my line."

"Everybody in Naconiche wants you to come back."

"Everybody?"

"Everybody I've talked to," he said. "Me most of all. Won't you consider it?" He gathered her into his arms and started to kiss her.

She held her face away. "Don't. I have a cold. You'll get germs."

"I don't care." He kissed her anyhow.

And what a wonderful kiss it was. She grew warm for the first time in days.

"Will you come back to us?" he asked. "I know you have to travel a lot, but we can work out something with your job. I know Naconiche isn't as exciting as Houston, but—"

She put her fingers over his lips. "I love Naconiche. I love the town. I love the people. I love you."

He flashed that killer smile. "Say that last part again."

"I love you."

He hugged her so hard he almost cracked her ribs. "God, I love to hear that. Say it again."

"I love you. And I'm tired of living in motel rooms. Think Naconiche can use another lawyer?"

"You betcha. Could I interest you in marrying the judge?"

"Sounds good to me."

When the maintenance man banged on the door a few minutes later, they ignored him. The room had grown plenty hot.

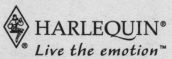

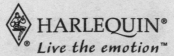

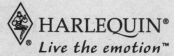

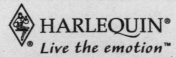